To
REIGN
for a thousand years

To Reign For A Thousand Years

RNWC Media, LLC
Imprint: "For His Glory"

Print: ISBN: 978-1-937975-31-9
Digital: ISBN: 978-1-937975-32-6

Preface

And he said to him, 'Well done, good servant! Because you have been faithful in a very little, you shall have authority over ten cities.'

Luke 19:17, English Standard Version

Then I saw thrones, and seated on them were those to whom the authority to judge was committed. Also I saw the souls of those who had been beheaded for the testimony of Jesus and for the word of God, and those who had not worshiped the beast or its image and had not received its mark on their foreheads or their hands. They came to life and reigned with Christ for a thousand years.

Revelation 20:4, English Standard Version

Contents

Preface

Contents

Restoration Begins

Prologue

"You do realize," said the teacher, peering at us over her gold-rimmed glasses, "you're in training to rule with Jesus. You understand that, right?"

It certainly says we'll rule with Him, I thought. But when, and where, and how? And ... we're in training for that?

"Every situation in your life, every frustration, every inconvenience, every disaster... every triumph and success ... is an opportunity for Him to teach you how to respond, how to walk with Him."

Just like Jesus did. Doing what we see Him doing. Saying what we hear Him saying. The 'mind of Christ,' they called it. Is that what I should be doing each day? How do you do that?

"We'll have a thousand years to put the world right again, with Satan locked up. Seems pretty clear. It's hard to know the sequence of events, of course ... prophecy never comes with a calendar, and a comma can be a millennium. But the description is clear. So how are we doing? Are we accepting the training?"

"Is this before Armageddon, or after?"

"When does 'the wedding of the Lamb' happen?"

We had a lot of questions, and of course people have been trying to sort all that out for a couple of thousand years now, so we weren't the first to ask such things.

"This particular passage seems to put them in this order," she said, running her finger down the page. "Armageddon ... then it says the time had come for the wedding feast, so I'm assuming the wedding itself happens about there ... then the thousand years begin. And I'm assuming that's at least part of the time for which we 'rule with Him'. And I'm also assuming — lots of assumptions here — that the parable about being faithful, and ruling over ten cities, etc, fits very well in that place. What do you think?"

Seemed reasonable to me.

I had always thought there were a lot of people and not enough cities for that calculation to work out ... but I also thought it wasn't just Earth we were talking about. That He made this universe to be thoroughly inhabited. And since He always seems to take the very small and mundane to start great things... Earth was as good a place to start as any.

So after He defeats every army on Earth at Armageddon, and the blood runs as deep as the horses' bridles, and the beast and false prophet are gone, and Satan is thrown into the abyss ... who's left?

This is apparently after massive catastrophes, as God shakes the foundations. Earthquakes, poison in the rivers, blood in the seas, mountains and islands removed from their places ... total disaster. Then, after ... after who knows how many years ... Armageddon.

If we're ruling with Him after that, and obviously are already in our permanent, eternal bodies ... who are we ruling over? Those who didn't come to the battle. And their children, and theirs?

Probably the beast and false prophet took total control of the Earth by then. Global government, all money replaced by electronic techniques, people totally enslaved to them ... and suddenly they're gone.

No money? Maybe no electricity? And very few people left?

What relationship do we offer these people as far as God is concerned? It's after the wedding of the Lamb, so ... the Bride of Christ, the church, is completed.

And the Jews are clearly the Bride of God, in Scripture, from long before the Christian church emerged.

Do the people living and being born after Armageddon now have an opportunity for a special relationship with the Holy Spirit? What an interesting idea!

It's not suggested anywhere ... but there was no hint of the Christian church era in the Old Testament, either. God is continually creative.

So perhaps we now begin ruling some number of cities, for a very long time, undoing the damage and offering choices. And eventually Satan is freed, and everyone has one last chance to choose their allegiance, and to withstand a final onslaught from the Deceiver.

"What do you think?" she repeated, and I realized I had been far away, trying to visualize the scene she was describing.

"Overwhelming," I said. Others nodded.

"How do the people then... fit into the picture?" I asked.

She looked around, and no one else offered an opinion.

"Consider the wedding banquet," she replied. "Who's there?"

"The king, so that's the Father."

"OK."

"The groom, so that's Jesus."

"I agree."

"The bride is there somewhere, so that's the church."

"Certainly a scriptural conclusion."

"And ... all those people who were invited, and all those people who were dragged in off the streets."

"And who are those people, really?" she asked. "Because the story seems to be all about them."

"Where is that, exactly?"

"Try Matthew's gospel. Matthew 22?" she said.

I scratched my head and stared at the page. Who were they, indeed?

Are these the people left after the wedding and after Armageddon? Healing from living under the counterfeit Jesus, and now beginning a brand new kind of relationship with God?

A normal world seemed to be going on, because those who didn't come were busy with normal things — farms and fields, business and family. But at the time of the wedding of the Lamb, so this had to be after what they call the 'rapture' ...

"Well, without sorting all that out, your point was that God is trying to train us for what comes next."

"Exactly," she said. "Exactly."

"So how does that work? What's your experience of it?"

"One aspect is that He doesn't care about results the way I do."

That was a bit unsettling. "So the way He fixes a problem may not be the way you would have fixed it."

"Or he may not fix it at all, by your definition. And you're left looking like a failure."

"So how is that ... you're saying that could be a successful lesson?"

"Sure. To those who loved Him, Jesus on the cross looked like total disaster. In reality, it was a complete triumph. Your letting someone cheat you, rather than taking them to court, might be a victory, according to Paul... but you could look like a fool to those who know you."

"I don't think I like this kind of training!"

She laughed. "I never do. Want another example?"

"Maybe," I said. "Go for it."

"Did you notice that Jesus would say one thing, then do another? Telling his followers He was not going to Jerusalem, for example, and going the next day?"

"Yes. what about that?"

"Since His own declaration was that He never did His own will, but only what the Father told Him to do... and told Him to say ... I assume His instructions changed."

"So He looked like a liar."

"Are you willing to look like a liar? Or a fool, or worse?"

I sat quiet for a minute. That was hard.

"What would He have us do, that would make us look like a fool?"

She smiled. "Can you think of anything He had the Old Testament prophets do that looked foolish, or dangerous, or crazy?"

"Just about everything!"

"Were they obeying Him?"

"Well, I think so. Sounds like it, even when it made no sense... except we get to see the end of the story, and often they were vindicated. Sometimes not."

She flipped some pages, and nodded. "So we need to be doing 'good works', according to Scripture. Do you know what those are?"

"Feeding the poor, being nice to people, being generous..."

"Those are christian things to do, if 'christian' is spelled with a lower case 'C' ... as C. S. Lewis would say."

"What do you mean?"

"Most religions would endorse those things. There's nothing particularly Christian about them."

"So... what does He want us to be doing?"

"Look up this phrase ... 'the works prepared beforehand, that we should walk in them.'"

"Oh, I know that one." I turned to it. "But what are those?"

"It's what He has prepared for you to do."

"But what is it? What are they?"

"Let me say it again ... what He has prepared for YOU to do."

I thought about it. "So, it might be different than what He has prepared for YOU to do."

"Exactly."

"And it might be very unpredictable."

"Just like everything He had Jesus and the prophets do."

"And it might never be the same way twice."

"Ditto."

"And He might tell you and me completely opposite things?"

"Like He apparently told Paul and Barnabas different things about John Mark."

"Yeah, they sure heard Him differently there ... but what if I'm trying to understand what He wants me to do, and I get it wrong?"

"Sounds like training, to me."

"What if people get hurt?"

"Your job is to obey, and forgive others. Their job is to obey, and forgive you."

My head was spinning. "How is this possible? How do we know what he wants us to do?"

"Jesus answered that question. Can you remember what He said?"

I took a deep breath, and tried to remember. "I think so. The Holy Spirit. 'He'll lead us into all truth.' Is that what you're thinking of?"

"Exactly. As far as walking that out, day by day, He showed us how. He said that He only did 'what He saw the Father doing.' Paul told the Corinthians that we 'have the mind of Christ.' Sounds like our walk should be the same as His."

"But what about the Bible?" I continued. "Isn't that how we know God?"

She smiled, and gave us time to think about it.

"That's certainly how I was raised. But what does the Scripture really say about itself?" she finally asked. "Paul wrote to Timothy that all Scripture is 'breathed out by God and profitable for teaching, for reproof, for correction, and for training in righteousness.' But does it take the place of the Holy Spirit, who leads us as Jesus said He would? In fact He leads us to Jesus, who is Truth, and 'in whom is the fullness of God'."

"That's a lot to think about."

"I agree," she said. "For a lifetime!"

Armageddon

He was magnificent, of course.

And the white stallion He rode was enormous, eager to be on the way, stamping and snorting. The battle for the future of Earth, and perhaps the universe, the battle prophesied for millennia, was gathering, and this horse couldn't wait.

I wondered if it was his bridles the Scripture was referring to? Blood would run six feet deep, if so.

The robes of the King were glowing, and the blood stains around the lower folds remained as an eternal reminder of the awful price He paid for us. Faithful and True. He certainly is. I love that name. And up the thigh, of course, in lettering that shimmers as though it's floating above the cloth, the robe declares Him to be King of All Kings and Lord of All Lords.

We gathered behind him, all on white horses that are everything their earthly cousins ever yearned to be. We were more than I could count, perhaps more than I could see. The armies of heaven had gathered to accompany "the last Adam" as He moved to reclaim what the first Adam gave away.

We begin moving away from the Thrones, outward from the pulsing light and glory of the Father's presence. It seemed as though the Universe were spread out before us, holding its breath, as we turned towards Earth.

We entered Earth's atmosphere. An angel rose up high above us, and he must have stood between the Earth and the sun, for his shadow was clearly visible on the face of the planet, and his voice echoed out across space and time. To those on Earth he must have looked like he was in the sun itself.

What was his message to the armies gathering on the plain of Megiddo? What could he say that would change their minds?

But instead of addressing them, he called to all the vultures of Earth to come for a feast, to gorge themselves on the kings and generals, the soldiers and horses and all who had gathered to defy King Jesus as He came to assert his authority.

Didn't those armies hear him? How could they not hear him? How could they still come, facing the one whose very breath is the sword of God?

Whether they heard him or not, they continued to gather in defiance, a vast spread of armies from the nations of the world. They had murdered God's people, hunting them down mercilessly, and now they would face their King.

'It is not the Father's will that any perish,' but apparently there finally comes an end, and on this day, for this army, that end arrived.

We must have looked like alien invaders to the earth-bound resistance, moving down from the heavens and spreading out in the sky above them.

The battle was brief. As John saw it from Patmos, so it was. The word of the King Himself went out as a sword from His mouth. It moved effortlessly through shields and armor, through weapons and vehicles. It hewed down all the flesh in the valley, from the least to the greatest.

There was far too much carnage to think of burials, and there was no one left to do the burying. The birds had to do the work, and it would take them far longer to clean up the mess than the battle itself lasted.

Then it was time for the ones called the beast and the false prophet, the ones who had done their best to counterfeit Jesus Himself and deceive many. The angel who had stood before the sun came to stand on the plain before them, with blood and death surrounding them all around, and seized them. Without a word he simply took hold of them, and a space opened up at his feet. It seemed a doorway from the physical world into another place, of which all I could see was fire. Even at a great distance, I felt the blistering heat of it on my face. The angel threw them into that opening, and it closed up before him. They were gone.

Then, as we watched, another angel came from the Throne with a great chain in his hand, and we saw Lucifer standing amid the uncountable bodies of those who had followed him. It was as though he had been there all along, but not apparent to our eyes, and now he was revealed.

The angel cast the chain around Lucifer and secured it; the devil was apparently unable to resist or flee.

A door stood before them, standing open. The angel threw the devil bodily through the opening, and pulled it closed. There was a great key on his sash, and he used it to secure the door.

He turned to us and said, "There he will remain for a thousand years." Then he was gone.

The hosts returned to great rejoicing in Heaven, and the wedding feast began.

Watching the Battle

The flat screen on the wall was amazing. The cameras couldn't get far enough back to show the whole army. All the armies, really. They covered the valley, and streamed in from every direction. Russia was there, and mighty Egypt, and what was left of France, and the Slovakia powerhouse, and Korea, and the Unified Army of South America, and the remnants of Eastern China. Too bad about the earthquakes. And the North America Forces, what was left after Yellowstone finally exploded. What a mess.

But there they were, gathered to face whatever challenge this was.

The leaders stood on a great stone in the center of the valley, looking at the sky. Cameras went back and forth from looking up, to looking at the vast sea of soldiers and vehicles. Laser tanks, nuclear rocket launchers, everything you could want was there to face this invading alien force. Now that war horses were back in style, they were everywhere. King Arthur would have loved to ride one of these, and to have the weapons in his hands that these soldiers had!

The news cameras had watched it for days, a host of creatures coming out of the deep heavens. From where? No one knew. They slowly gathered, and seemed as many as the stars themselves when you looked up at night. In fact, the stars had just about disappeared, with these creatures in the way.

But the Leaders were calling the whole world to battle, to defend us against the alien forces. It was like we had known for hundreds of years they were coming. All the movies, all the books, everything warned us — this would come, and it would be a desperate situation, but we would win out. We always won out. So it would happen again.

I shifted my leg on the cushion. Finally beginning to heal, it was shattered from falling at the transformer factory. Didn't know a leg could go into that many pieces and still be put back together! And the hip, for that matter. And the artificial spine. Amazing stuff, I have no idea how they could do that, but ... here I am, and insurance paid it all.

Be glad to not need the narcotics anymore to get through the day.

Kept me from being in the battle. Wished I could have gone. That must have been an amazing sight in person.

The camera switched again to the skies, and zoomed in as tight as they could on the leader. He seemed to have crowns on his head, and everyone with him rode white horses. The soldiers beside him seemed to glow, and behind them were ... at least thousands, if not thousands of thousands of soldiers, all on those horses. And the horses seemed decorated for a party, not like you would outfit them for a bloody war. Still hard to see, at that distance, but it seemed odd.

And the soldiers, for that matter... they did not seem to be holding or waving any weapons. Just sat on their horses, looking at us, and getting closer.

I pushed up from the couch, and glided into the kitchen on the new megawatt glider. Just a touch, just a bit of a shift of my weight, and it knew exactly what I wanted. Nice. They had them on sale the next week at SuperMart. I thought I should get a couple for the kids.

Foamed up a drink and some frozen cream, and slid back across the living room to the couch. As I lay back into the recliner, I realized the picture had changed. The images were much bigger. They were coming in. Must have been about noon there, half a world away... but now the brightness of the aliens was making it hard for the cameras. Glare was everywhere.

It looked like their king moved down ahead of the rest, and came to stand his horse on the valley floor about a hundred yards from the Leaders. What was he doing? Didn't he understand the power of the Leaders? They did miracles! One of them had come back from the dead!

They began talking, but it was strange. There was no sound that the microphones could pick up, and those had to be great microphones! But as the whole valley strained to hear what was being said, there was only the wind picking up, and the stamping of horses, and men shifting their feet as they waited.

Why didn't someone just nuke the guy, and be done with it?

Then something amazing happened. One of the aliens came to the rock, one of the big glowing men. He tossed a rope, or chain, or something around the Leaders, and tied them up like you had wrapped them in duct tape. They could not move, they were obviously being held against their will, but apparently could do nothing.

Then the alien king spoke ... the cameras were on him, so we saw him speak, but it wasn't words that came out. It was ... it was like a laser, or something far more powerful. It was like a great sword, and it simply swept across the valley, and everyone fell, animals and men alike. Blood was everywhere. And when it came around to where the cameras were, they suddenly lurched and never moved again. One of them was still pointed at the platform, and I could see the Leaders still held there. When it looked like nothing else in the entire valley was left alive, at least the part I could see, the alien king pointed to the Leaders and they just ... it wasn't like they went somewhere else, or disappeared, they ... evaporated. Turned into smoke and drifted away.

So at the end it was that simple, and they were gone. They controlled the whole world, and made everyone be tattooed in order to buy food, or anything else. They had shut down all governments, all money, all networks, all everything, and just run it all themselves.

And now they were ... gone.

Then another creature appeared in front of the alien king. A giant serpent, covered in jewels, and awful to look at. The leaders must have been working for him. The glowing man threw a chain around him too, and a doorway opened into blackness ... the camera was looking right at it, right into it, and there was nothing there. And the man threw the huge snake into the door, and closed it, and seemed to lock it with a huge key.

So that's why none of the aliens were carrying weapons. They didn't need any!

Then the birds came. Vultures, buzzards, and every kind I'd ever seen or heard of, I guess. Millions of them. And they came like they had been called, right on time... and as rivers of blood ran through the valley, they settled in for a feast.

No way to bury all those men and beasts. No place. And no one to do it.

Then the alien king simply turned and rode back into the sky. There was no one to turn the cameras, so we couldn't see what happened next, but ... he was gone. And the cameras just watched the birds... until the power ran out, I guess. I turned it off, amazed.

What would happen next? The Leaders had taken control of the world, and nothing happened without their approval.

I changed to a news program coming from my city, and the cameras just looked at the announcers, and they just looked at each other and the camera. They had all seen just what I did, and their heads were spinning just like mine.

I turned off the lights and went to bed. I didn't know how to even think about it, and they sure didn't.

In the morning the electricity was off. I had to find the emergency book to figure out how to get out of the house... electricity never went off, so everything was built to depend on it. But there was a pull string on the back of the lock over the main door, and I pulled it, and the lock popped open. Must have been an old one, or that string wouldn't have been there. I think the Leaders wouldn't allow such things. Would have suggested a lack of faith in their ... systems ... probably could have gotten you killed, to put such a thing in a product these days. They were serious ... had been serious ...

I stepped out into the morning sunshine. My neighbor's wife was standing on her sidewalk looking up. I looked up too, but there was nothing to see. I walked over to her.

"Jessie."

She finally looked at me, with a completely blank expression. Finally she said, "They're gone."

And I realized she wasn't just talking about the Leaders. She was talking about her husband, and every other man on this street, all of whom had gone to war. All of whom had proudly worn their uniforms and their tattoos, and answered the summons to protect the Earth from alien invaders.

And they were gone.

I wrapped my arms around her, and after a minute or two she began to cry. We stood like that for a while.

Then I stepped back, and she said, "What will we do? What happens now?"

I shrugged. "Get together with everyone. Start talking about it."

She pointed to the house behind her. "The power is off. All the food will spoil. The power toilets won't flush, the cookers won't cook, the ... when the pressure goes down, there won't even be any water."

She began to cry again, and I realized I was in the same situation. We all were. What would we do? How would we eat?

I gathered her in my arms again, and I held her until the sobs stopped. Then we simply walked back into our houses, still trying to just think about the situation through the fog of complete amazement.

The Wedding

The Bride of God, Israel, was there, having been restored as Paul said she would be. The Bride of Christ gathered, and the garments we each wore were spectacular. They represented the "good deeds" of the people of God, which simply meant the works He had prepared beforehand for us to walk in. How could they not be fabulous?

The innumerable wedding guests were each given a garment, as was traditional in the Jewish weddings, and it seemed to me that many of them were surprised to have been invited; indeed, some looked as though the angels had literally dragged them in. The second resurrection had not yet happened, and many still lived on earth; perhaps the Father brought all who were still alive, in the spirit or in the flesh, I could not say, to attend the wedding. We who had already died in Christ, and those who had been caught up with Jesus in the air, formed the Bride.

But one man appeared in the midst of the guests without the required garment. How had he gotten in without accepting his garment of grace, given freely to all who would receive it? It was an insult to the groom, to not wear the beautiful garment offered to each guest!

He was taken to the Father, and apparently thrown out for his rebellion.

The high point of the feast was when Jesus took a cup, filled it with wine, and said, "I have waited long to drink this with you again." Tears flowed. Much had happened since the night He was referring to, and He had indeed waited long.

The wedding brought a level of intimacy with the King even beyond that of the indwelling Spirit, and the deeper kind of commitment to move in shared goals and priorities that any good earthly marriage would understand. Communication with Him in the Spirit is far closer and instinctive, now that we share the kind of glorified body that the disciples saw in Jesus after the resurrection. But we still walk as He did then, doing and saying what the Father is doing and saying. As we moved into our ruling positions, that would be crucial.

The parable of the talents told the whole story. We've got a thousand years to straighten things out, before Satan is loosed again. Will the surviving population of earth, and those to come, work with us or need the "iron rod" to manage them?

Free will is the Father's eternal gift, and each one made in His image gets to choose. So do those not made in His image, like the angels; He lets each make their own choice about their relationship with Him. Long before Adam, Satan's rebellion threw Heaven into open war; it appears that some will still reject God until the end, when the new Heaven and the new Earth replace what we have known.

But for now, we have a thousand years of work to do.

Restoration Begins

Restonia

I arrived in Restonia a year after the battle at Armageddon.

I walked into town from the south, coming first to farms and scattered homes, and then into small paved streets with neighborhoods off to each side. People seemed to walk furtively, quickly, avoiding eye contact, as though conversation would be dangerous.

It must have been a city of a few million before the battle. I imagined the bustle, the activity, before so many left for the fight and never returned. The grief must have been overwhelming, when the news came. Of course, they would have seen it on worldwide displays, everyone would have watched. In horror.

As the neighborhoods gave way to abandoned industrial buildings, there were fewer people about. I came to a street corner where a tall, thin young man leaned against a lightpole and watched me approach. As I came, he shifted his stance to face me, and stood with both hands at his side, as though expecting to counter an attack of some kind.

"Hello," I said.

"You look weird," he said. "Where you from?"

"How do I look weird?"

"Them clothes, man. You look like them aliens that killed all our people. You remember that?"

"I remember," I said. "You thought those were aliens?"

"Of course. I've seen the movies. 'Cept we were s'posed to win, we always did in the movies."

I nodded. "What's your name?"

"Sammy. Yours?"

"James," I said. "You can call me 'James'."

"What do you mean? Not really your name?"

"I think it is. Haven't used it since ... a long time."

"So why you dressed so funny ... James?"

I looked at my robe, and looked at his clothes. Quite a difference.

"Where can I get some better stuff?"

He pointed across the street. "Second-hand shop. Leftover stuff. Still open for another few minutes. Come on, I'll show you where stuff is that would fit you."

"Thanks." We walked across the street, so little traffic you didn't have to worry about looking both ways. I smiled at the memory of that simple routine, from another life.

I pushed open the door and got stares from two clerks at the cash registers, both leaning against their counters with nothing to do. "Yeah, you need some clothes!" laughed one. "My daughter would love that gown!"

Sammy shoved me back to the rack on the far left. "You look like about this size," he said, pulling some jeans from the shelf. "What size belt you wear?"

I shrugged. "No idea."

"I'll guess a 40. Here. Got any underwear under that dress?"

"Nope."

He tossed me a pair of boxer shorts, some flip flops, and a T-shirt that said "Make Your Own Future!" Waving towards a door at the back, he said, "Go change clothes back there."

I looked behind him at Arul, the angel that had followed me in, and tilted my head to invite him to join me. "Back in a minute," I said to Sammy, as the angel walked into the dressing room ahead of me.   Inside, I took off the robe, handed it to him, and climbed into the left over clothes.

He smiled. "Look OK?" He smiled bigger, and nodded, but said nothing. I motioned "shhh" to him, and walked out.

"Good," said Sammy. "Very nice," said the clerk. "You busy tonight?"

I laughed. "I'm going to be busy for a very long time! Thanks for asking. But I have no money to pay for this. What can we do?"

"You'll have to work it off, I guess," said the other clerk. "What can you do?"

"I can pray."

"Pray? Pray for what? To who?"

"To God. For whatever you need."

"You're weird, man. Tell you what. Pray to get rid of this headache I've got, and you are paid ... in ... full ... if it goes away."

"Is that all?"

"Is that all? Easy for you, and a good deal for me! And nothin' gonna happen, anyway!"

"Your name is Sheila, isn't it?"

She stared.

"How about if I pray for your runaway daughter to come home, too?"

Tears filled Sheila's eyes. "Don't mess with me! You don't know me! How do you know about her?"

"I know that God loves you, and loves her, and He tells me your heart is broken over this. But she's OK, and we can ask Him to send her back. Sound good?"

She nodded, tears flowing. The other clerk came and hugged her, with pure anger in her eyes for my causing the pain she saw. "You better not be messing with her, or I'll ..."

I held out my hand to Sheila, and she took it.

"Jesus, thank you for showing me what Sheila needs. I ask healing for this headache, and for ... Sandra? ... to come home safely."

Behind her, a small voice said, "Mama?"

Sheila whirled, stood motionless for a moment, then she and her friend both ran to the door and hugged the young lady who stood there clutching a sweater.

Sammy came up close, and whispered, "Let me guess. The headache is gone too."

I winked at him and nodded. "I think we can go now."

***

On the street, Sammy suddenly stopped and said, "Where's that dress you were wearing?"

I looked down at my clothes, looked at my empty hands, and shrugged. "Did you want it?"

"It was kinda nice, except for bein' a dress. You could'a sold it for somethin'!"

"Naw, that's fine. It's getting dark. I don't have a place to stay. Guess I'll keep walking. The city that way?"

"Hey, man, you don't wanna walk up that way at night. I got a couch you can crash on. Up this way," he motioned to a side street. "Couple blocks."

As we climbed some wooden steps up the back side of a rundown frame house, he said, "You know, I could knock you over and rob you, 'cept you got nothin'. Ain't you scared of being beat up, or somethin'?"

"No, not so much. Are you?"

"Not me. That's why I pack this," and he patted a lump under his T-shirt. No one gonna mess with me."

He poured some leftover coffee into a couple of cups and put them in a microwave. "Made it this morning, should still be good." He cocked an eyebrow at me to see if I disagreed. "You want sugar?"

"Sure," I said, and waited for him to sit down.

"You ever hear of Jesus, Sammy?"

"Only when I curse. Is that a real person?"

"Yeah, He is. He's God's son, and He owns the planet. I've been adopted into the family, and He sent me to help get this part of it working right again."

Sammy threw his head back and laughed, and laughed some more. "You are right out of the looney bin, you really are!"

I took a sip of the coffee. Pretty strong.

"Ask me something."

"Like what?"

"Anything you think I don't know, something that there's no way I could know it."

"Why?"

"I want to show you that I'm telling the truth... that God sent me."

"No. No clues. You tell me something, and I'll tell you if you're right."

"You're carrying an old Glock 27, .40 caliber, with 6 shells in it. You stole it from a guy called Viper, and he's really the reason you keep it ready."

Sammy froze, his coffee cup at his mouth. He slowly lowered it to the table, as though he thought it would jump from his hand if he lost control.

"What else?"

"You live here because the man living with your Mom can't stand you, and she won't leave him."

"I'm getting really angry," said Sammy after a quiet moment staring at the table. "You better leave."

"What's really important," I said gently, "is that Jesus sent me to introduce you to Him, and set you free from all the anger and pain that has filled your heart. He paid the price for all that ... for everything you've done, and everything that's been done to you. And he wants you to come home."

Sammy sat with his hands clenched for a long time, then said again, very slowly, "You need to leave."

I stood up. "You've been kind to me, and helped me a lot. When you want to talk, you'll be able to find me." He did not look up.

I closed the door behind me, and stood there for a moment. Sammy cursed once, and then I heard him begin to weep. I walked down the stairs, two blocks back to the main road, and started towards town. The road angled to the right, and the stars were coming out over tall buildings ahead as I walked. There were few lights, and the stars were bright until the moon began rising on my right.

Making Friends

How do we lead our cities to know Him? How do we act as shepherds, as suffering servants, kings and priests, working with rebellious subjects to set the world right again? Not to mention working in the knowledge that the Evil One will be set free again at the end of it, to give our realms a final choice?

A thousand years may go by pretty quickly!

I had not yet seen a car, or whatever they use for vehicles in this era. Electricity is working; is gasoline? Did the massive reduction in humanity at Armageddon set back those who were left, in every aspect of daily life?

What year was it, Earth time? I wasn't sure. Had no idea, actually, except that Sammy's English seemed about the same as I remembered. Or perhaps I would have understood whatever language he spoke. I had died in the twenty-first century... but time had passed on Earth, while I had been in Heaven. How much time?

As the moon rose, I noticed that the street seemed more like a walkway than a driving path. Stones, bits of litter, a bench here and there ... you wouldn't leave those things where cars would be coming.

I arrived in a park, as the moon was high above. A lake spread out in the center of it, and tables with small benches were scattered under ancient oaks and maples. Since leaving

Sammy I had not seen a single person, and I wondered why he had warned me about walking this way at night.

I sat on a table at the edge of the lake and watched the ripples of moonlight on the water. The moon's light obscured the stars and threw deep shadows under the trees, with pale, crisp light on the grass and walkways.

I felt someone approaching, and turned around on the table to see. Four shapes came out of the shadows towards me, all walking slowly and staying widely separated.

"Hello," I said.

There was no response.

"Arul, can they see you?"

A brilliant light shone from just behind me, and the four young men, for that they were, fell backwards onto the ground. The light was suddenly gone, and I laughed. "I guess they did!"

Certainly blinded for a few moments, they struggled to their feet and looked around.

The tallest finally spoke. "Who was that?"

"His name is Arul," I said. "He stands by the throne of God, in light more fiery than the sun, so he hides himself most of the time... out of kindness, you understand."

Silence. They could probably see fairly well, by now, but came no closer.

"And you?"

"James. Where do you boys live?"

"Don't call me a boy, mister," said the one to my right. "I'm full grown fifteen years, and I'd whup you if that fire man would let me."

"Come here, Jonathan," I said, and he exclaimed. "How did you... ?"

I sat down on the bench behind the table. "Come put your elbow here, and take my hand, and see if you can do a simple thing... push my hand down to the table."

"Yeah, JJ, you show him, you go do it!" hollered the others. "You put him right, you show 'im!"

Jonathan slowly came to the table and sat down opposite me. Nervous and watchful, he was being tested in front of his friends, and being full of pride there was no way he would refuse the test.

We clasped hands, and I began praying for him. As he pushed hard, I felt the Spirit moving through the contact, and I whispered, "God has forgiven you for everything. He wants you to come home."

The pressure on my hand intensified, if that were possible, and the spirit of rebellion rose to fill his eyes and expression.

"You are completely forgiven," I whispered. "You can be free."

His eyes were wet now, and of course he had not budged my hand at all, with every ounce of his strength. "I know you need to win, so I'll let you," I whispered. "It's our secret!" And I let my hand slowly lower, as his friends cheered him on. Finally he had me on the table, and stood in triumph with arms raised. But he did not walk away; instead, he slowly sat back down and looked at me.

"Where you from?" he said, quietly.

"I live here now," I said. "Except I don't have a place yet."

"You can be with us," he said. "Guys ... ", he said, louder, "James is gonna join us. And the fire man, too."

"Right?" he asked me.

"He and I travel together," I nodded. "But he doesn't take any room, and we don't eat much."

"You're weird," said JJ, shaking his head. "But I like you."

He turned and pointed to the guys around him. "Steve, Jimmy, Tank."

Then he pointed back at me. "James."

And that seemed to settle it.

We walked in silence another few blocks to the north, without seeing anyone. Finally I asked, "Where is everyone?"

"Everyone hides at night. Except us."

But it seemed to me they were walking very quietly, and watching in every direction.

"What about in the daytime?"

"Mostly the men are gone. They went to the war, and never came back."

"And their families?"

"We look after them."

"Who is we?"

He looked at me and kept walking. "I'll show you. There's a meeting tomorrow."

We came to a high-rise apartment building with no lights at all. The door was ajar into the main downstairs hallway, and we entered the building. To the right was a stairwell, and we turned into it.   At each landing a candle burned, and we climbed six flights.

"You're in good shape!" said JJ. "I don't even see you breathing hard!"

"Thanks," I said. "Been living in a high place, not much oxygen."

"Heard about that," he said. "You can run further that way, huh?"

"I suppose so."

As we came out onto the sixth floor, JJ led the way into the first apartment on the right. It must have been expensive, when the city was full. A wonderful balcony opened over the city view, and there were rooms opening in every direction.

"We can't pay for electricity, so we use candles," he said. "Most people do. You hungry?"

"No, I'm good. Go ahead and eat. Can I sit here and look at the city?" He nodded, and I settled into an easy chair. The moon was going down behind us, and the remaining light was full on the buildings and streets below.

JJ sat down on the floor in the middle of the room. Steve, Jimmy, and Tank flopped down on couches around us.

"So. Who are you, really? No one walks into town with no place to stay, in the middle of the night."

"First, tell me about the war. Did you see the big battle?"

"When everyone got killed? Yeah. On the big screens."

He motioned, and I saw a video display of some sort that filled an entire wall.

"Did you see the ones coming down from the sky?"

He shivered. "Creepy. Scary stuff."

"Do you know who they were?"

"Space men. Aliens, from other planets. What else?" Tank was quite certain of this.

"Did you see the one in front, on the big horse, with eyes like fire and wearing crowns?"

"I did," said JJ. "He was running the outfit, wasn't he?"

He looked at me intently. "Where were you when that happened?"

"I was with him."

There was silence for a long time. "And the fire man, too?" asked Steve, who had not spoken all night.

"Yes."

"That's crazy! How do we know you're telling the truth," asked Tank. "They came out of the sky!"

"How did I know JJ's name?" Silence again.

Finally I asked, "Did you see what happened to the beast and the false prophet?"

"Who?"

"The guys who had been doing miracles, and making everyone get branded with their number, and killing anyone who wouldn't."

"No. Were they there? It all went black when your big guy … killed everyone."

"They're gone. Forever."

"Oh, man, that's a rip! They were going to make everything right. Peace, no fighting, everyone would have plenty to eat, good stuff all around. And they're gone?"

"They were lying," I said. "Nothing but slavery was ahead."

"And now we got space aliens instead?" demanded Tank. "Where did they go, anyway? After it all went dark."

"The 'big guy' is Jesus. He's God's son. And all the kings of the planet were there to fight Him. He offered them forgiveness ... like he does you ... but they would have none of it, and finally He had to wipe them out."

"What do you mean, forgiveness?" asked Jimmy. "From what? We never did anything to him! Never even seen him!"

"Ever hurt anyone?"

"Well, sure."

"Ever lied?"

Jimmy laughed. "Who hasn't?"

"Ever hated anyone?"

After a pause, "Yeah."

"You want me to go on?" I asked. "It's a long list."

"So how come this guy is the one who forgives people? Bet no one ever treated him bad!"

"Wait," said JJ. "You mean 'Jesus,' like 'Jesus Christ'?"

I nodded, then realized they probably did not see me nod, in the dark of the apartment. "That's Him."

"So, like, the guy they crucified?"

"For you. In your place. To pay your punishment, for all the stuff we could list... except we don't have to. It's gone."

"But he's dead! A jillion years ago!"

"Was dead. Is King. You saw Him."

"That was him? And you know Him?"

"You asked me a while ago, 'Who are you, really?'"

"Yup."

"He sent me to you, to introduce you to Him. To invite you to join the family."

"This is too crazy for me," said Tank. "I'm gonna crash." And he stood up, stretched, and walked into one of the adjoining rooms.

"What if we hadn't found you in the park," asked Jimmy, yawning. "What if we'd just beat you up and taken whatever you had? Oh, yeah, the fire man. But what if that never happened?"

"You think it was an accident?"

Breakfast

The sun was well up when they stirred and wandered back into the main room.

Jimmy looked out at the balcony and shouted, "Hey! You! Get back!"

I turned to look at him. "Is something wrong?"

"You're too close to the edge! You could fall, man!"

I looked down, and saw that I was, in fact, at the edge, and I could tell he was almost frantic about it.

"Sorry, Jimmy. Enjoying the view. Is this better?"

I stepped back a few paces, and he nodded. "Yeah, man, that's better. What were you thinking? That you can fly?"

I wasn't sure what to say. Need to be more aware of how people feel about things, when they're still in their mortal bodies. How I used to feel ... so long ago.

I guess Jesus had the same transition, when He strolled down the beach and made a fish breakfast for his old friends, or on the Emmaus road, or in the room when he showed them his wounds. Looked the same to them. Wasn't the same.

"I'll be careful, Jimmy. Thanks."

Tank wandered out. "You still here? Beginning to think you was a dream. Did you make us some breakfast?"

"No... is it my turn?"

"Yeah, the new guy makes breakfast. And it's about time, I can't take much more of those pancakes Jimmy's been making!"

Jimmy threw a pillow at him, and I could tell this was a long, long conversation.

"What do you have?"

"Tank waved at the refrigerator. "Eggs, bacon, beer ... hey, JJ, what else we got to eat? New guy is gonna feed us!"

"Oatmeal," came the muffled, pillow-buried voice from the far bedroom. "Lots and lots of oatmeal, since you guys don't like it!"

"Oatmeal," I said. "Haven't had that in a long time!"

"Oooh," groaned Tank. "He's gonna make oatmeal."

I pulled cabinet doors open until I found it. JJ was right; there was a lot.

"OK, how about a pot to cook it in?"

"Under the counter, over there." Tank was not happy.

By the time they came to the table, the oatmeal had raisins, cinnamon, brown sugar, chopped pecans, milk, and sliced bananas. With a fresh pot of coffee to replace the beer.

"What the .... Where'd you get all that stuff?"

"Try it. See if you like it this way."

As they pulled up chairs, I said, "Mind if I say grace?"

They looked at each other. "Say what? You can say anything you want, I guess!"

"Sorry. It means to thank God for the food we have to eat."

"God didn't get that. I stole the sugar from Thompson, and ..."

I waved my hand. "I'm sorry for Thompson, I guess, but if it weren't for God's love for you, you wouldn't have clothes to wear or food to eat or a bed to sleep in. Who do you think sends the rain to grow this wonderful oatmeal?"

"You're weird," said Jimmy. "You sound like all those Christians that disappeared. My uncle was like that, until they shot him for not getting the tattoo. Talked about God."

I looked up through the ceiling towards the sky; somehow it seemed right, even though Heaven isn't really up there. Then I decided just looking at the food would be fine. "Thank you, Father, and I ask your blessing for my friends and this city."

They just listened, then went to eating without comment. I filled a big bowl. Best I'd had in ... well, who knows? You lose track of time, up there.

"You really like this stuff, don't you?" asked JJ.

"Is it OK?"

He took a bite. "Hey, this ain't bad! Take some, Tank, make a believer outta you!"

"Not likely," he said, but I noticed there were no complaints as he consumed a pretty good helping.

"So what is this meeting you were talking about?" I asked, when the bowls were mostly empty.

"City meeting, what's left of us. Everyone comes, those who can, and the ones we send do all the talking."

"Who do you send?"

"From this part of town, Frank goes. You'll meet him."

"Why him?"

"He wants to be the one. And he's bigger than anyone else, so he pretty much gets what he wants."

"Why didn't he go to the war?"

"His left arm doesn't work. Got a knife in it when he was a kid, and ... just doesn't work. So didn't have to go."

"Why didn't you guys go?"

There was silence around the table, and I knew the answer. "They didn't come find you, and drag you along?"

For the first time, Steve spoke up, in a quiet, soft voice. "They said they would deal with us when they got back," he said. "It was going to be awful."

I nodded. No doubt about that.

"What will they talk about at the meeting?"

"The talkers decide about things," said JJ. "Whatever needs deciding about. We just go to know what's goin' down, and besides, it's fun. Sometimes. When it's not boring."

"Where's your fire man?" whispered Steve. "Is he still here?"

I pointed to Arul, standing on the balcony. "Out there. He likes being in the sun."

Arul turned and smiled at me. Our joke.

"Why can't we see him?"

"Because he's not really there," said Tank. "It's a joke."

"Because he's an angel," I said, "and most people are a little nervous having him around. He's a big guy. You fell on the ground when you first saw him, remember?"

"We didn't see no whatever-you-said," Tank scoffed. "You made some big light shine, and it surprised us. Some magic trick, or gunpowder."

Arul shrugged, and turned back to watch the city.

"Does he know this Jesus person too?" asked JJ.

"Very well," I said, "and for a very long time."

"So did you say why you came?" asked Jimmy. "I don't remember the answer... and you just walked into town last night, from ... where?"

I was about to answer when a blast of noise came from the balcony, and I looked at where Arul had been standing. There was no sign of him. I went to the balcony and looked around the city, but could not see him anywhere.

"Lose something?" asked JJ.

They had not heard the sound, and of course did not know that Arul had left.

"Arul's gone," I said. "Just left, in a hurry. I was trying to see if I could tell what was going on."

"Yeah, yeah," said Tank. "Next you'll tell us you have an army floating in the sky, ready to hit the streets when you need them."

I smiled. It was tempting, I admit.

"When should we leave for the meeting?" I asked.

"We can go now," said Jimmy. "Plenty of time, but sometimes there's some action before the Talkers get started."

"Yeah," said Tank. "And maybe it will be us!"

The others cheered, but Steve was barely audible. Deeply wounded, I felt, but he might be strong when all that is healed.

The Talkers

As we walked towards the tallest buildings, others began to appear. None of them walked close to us, or made eye contact.

"Who keeps the electricity going?" I asked Steve, when I noticed a lit sign in a small shop.

"Whoever the Talkers tell to do it," he said.

"What if they can't, or don't, or want to do something else?"

"That's not so good," Steve said, looking down. "Not many refuse."

"How do people pay for the electricity? That shop, for example... I get the feeling it's expensive. Can they afford it?"

"Pay?" asked Steve. "What do you mean, 'pay for it'?"

"Do you have money, what people give you for doing work for them, and then you use that to trade it for what you want — food, shoes, clothes ...?"

He shook his head.

"Don't work that way. You do what the Talkers tell you to, and they make people give you electricity, if they think you should have it. One of the Talkers has that shop, so he gets whatever he wants."

He glanced back at it. "Don't go there, James. People go in there and never come out, some of them."

A large park in the middle of the city seemed to be the meeting place, and hundreds were sitting around on the grass when we arrived. As my friends and I walked into the grassy area, people stood up and moved out of our way.

"Why are they doing that?" I asked.

"Doing what?," asked Tank. "Getting out of our way?"

"Yes, that."

"Because we're with Frank, and they know it. Nobody gonna cross Frank."

A platform that might have been for bands to play and children to run was now where the Talkers would have their say. Three people were on the stage when we arrived, and we sat down about twenty feet away. Every now and then another person would climb up on the stage and take one of the dozen chairs scattered about.

I stood up and began to walk away from the group. JJ spoke up.

"James!"

"What?"

"Don't wander off."

"Thought I'd go meet some people, see what's going on."

"No. Only their Talker can talk to them. You can't. You're with us, and they know it. No one will talk to you."

"Not even more of Frank's people?"

"Ain't none here. We come, no one else does."

"I'll be fine," I said, and began walking among the other people. They stared at me, and no one made an effort to speak or greet me.

I saw a young mother holding a flushed, crying baby, trying to quiet it. The fever was obvious, and so was her lack of medicine. I walked to her, knelt down, and said, "I'm going to ask God to heal your daughter. May I touch her?"

The mother looked intently at me, and clutched the baby even tighter. She finally made the tiniest of motions, nodding a "Yes" to my question. I put a hand on the child's foot and said, "Father, please heal this child."

The crying stopped instantly. As the mother and I watched, the color of her face receded to a normal pink, she looked at her mother's face, and relaxed into sleep.

"She'll be fine now," I said. "God loves you both."

Then I stood and walked a little further. A commotion on the stage caught my attention, and I looked to see a large man pointing at me and shouting at the crowd. Shouting at my friends, I realized.

And I saw Arul standing just beyond the large man, watching him.

Seemed like a good time to return to my group. The young mother smiled at me as I walked back past her.

"Something wrong?" I said to JJ, who was standing and facing the screaming man. He did not turn to face me, and in fact, seemed to be afraid to do so.

I turned towards the stage and walked to it. The screaming Talker shifted his focus to me, and the intensity of his voice increased. I raised a hand in his direction and said, "Be quiet."

He stopped in mid-sentence, if you could call his raging "sentences." His face remained red, his eyes furious, but no words came out. The others on the stage stared at me.

"You may continue," I said to them in the total silence. "Go on with your meeting. Perhaps your friend will be able to join you later."

Then I went back to our group and sat next to JJ's feet. Eventually he sat down next to me and stared at my face from a few inches away.

"How did you do that?" he whispered. "Why did you do that? That's Frank. He was just mad 'cause you broke the rules, like I told you, you can't go talk to people."

"Do you think that's a good rule, JJ?"

"I ... a good rule? It's the rule. What do you mean, is it a good rule?"

"Not any more," I said, and turned to watch the meeting.

After three hours of rambling discussion of a wide range of subjects, with no obvious decisions and no apparent way to implement any decision that was made, they seemed on the verge of ending the "meeting." Much of the conversation was between individuals, and only partly audible to the crowd, but there was no motion among the assembled listeners to either leave or get involved.

Frank sat on the edge of the group, apparently resigned to not having a voice for the moment, and occasionally glared at me.

I stepped up onto the platform and stood at the edge of the group, waiting. One by one they noticed me, and eventually the various conversations stopped and they looked my way.

"Frank, you may speak now," I said to him, and his face relaxed in a way that few would have noticed. He tentatively responded, "OK ... OK." And said no more.

The group was quite a mixture — all ages, both sexes, various races.

"Please introduce yourselves," I said. "Who are you, what group or part of town do you represent, why are you here ... what do you hope for, when you come here?"

I pointed to a young lady on my left, and waved in a circle around the group to suggest an order of participation. She stood, looked about as though for permission, and then back to me.

She stood tall, as an athlete would, and comfortably balanced. Perhaps accustomed to public speaking, she seemed completely at ease before the crowd.

"The northeast of the city, from the old highway up to where the river crosses. My family lived there, and farmed, before the war. I'm the oldest of four, and now represent the families left there.

"What do I hope for? Some sort of social order ... some understanding of what we do next. Some healing of grief."

She looked around again, and added, "And these are my friends." She sat down.

An older man next to her stood up stiffly, and I thought him to be about 70, though his hair was still black and he needed no cane.

"Not many can make the trip," he said, "so I come. Want to stay in touch with what is happening, learn what I can, and try to help the families in the York section. Couldn't make the trip to the battle, so I'm still here, and can barely make this trip... but it's worth it. As Ann said, these folk have become friends."

"Oh," he added. "You can call me Jackson. And what's your name, by the way?"

"You can call me James," I replied. "Thank you. And you?" I pointed to the next man beyond Jackson.

A wiry older fellow stood, with an easy smile and a friendly face. Seemed to be the kind of man who could probably fix anything, advise anyone, and lead any group.

"I'm HL," he said. "Live on the far east side, past the old tracks. Like they said, we're trying to find our way now that all the leaders have gone. I was a lawyer, but it's not so clear now what the law is, or who would enforce it. But it's interesting, there's not so much crime going on now, as though whatever drives that has gone on vacation."

"Thank you, HL. And Jackson, and Ann. Let me explain that, for just a moment. You saw the battle, but apparently you did not see what happened next. The two men who had been doing miracles, and making people get marked or tattooed, and one of them had come back from the dead... they are gone."

Suddenly the crowd was a sea of tumult, and everyone exclaimed to their neighbor.

"That's why there's a peace in the air that was not there before. You can feel it, I'm sure."

Many nodded, and sounds of agreement moved across the park.

"The one you saw coming down from the sky, leading the army on white horses?" Angry murmurs emerged.

"You were taught to fear him, but you should not. He came to set you free. It is by his power that those deceivers are gone, and he has also imprisoned Lucifer ... you may have heard Christians speak of the devil, or Satan ... he is now locked up for a long time."

I waited a few moments, as they reacted to all this.

"So the deceivers had swept away all the systems, all the laws and normal practices of running your government, and become dictators. But they are gone, and it falls to us now to rebuild our cities, and more, to restore the planet... heal some longstanding wounds."

Now I waited. That was a lot to absorb, and I was sure questions would come. They did.

"So, how do we know you're not a deceiver, and you're lying to us about all of this?"

"That's a great question, Cindy. It is Cindy, right?"

She nodded, eyebrows raised.

"How can I prove it to you? The deceivers showed you miracles, so if I do things that seem magical, that does not prove anything. What proof would be good enough?"

They began talking among themselves, and it became obvious there was nothing I could do that would be conclusive.

"And then you'd have to go back to your people and tell them, and then it's just hearsay and rumor, so they won't believe you. Right?

Nods of agreement.

"Here's the problem. The God who made us all has shown his love for you, and the Jesus you saw leading that army gave His life for you. He did all sorts of miracles, and was killed, and rose from the dead. God did everything possible to demonstrate that Jesus was from Him.

"Now he has defeated those who counterfeited all He did, deceiving you with miracles and resurrection both, and He has given us freedom. What will you do with it?"

I waited a moment. "Did the deceivers leave you free to live your lives?"

"Yes," said Frank, regaining some of his anger. "As long as we did what they said, we could do whatever we wanted."

I looked around at the group. "Listen to what he said. As long as you were completely obedient slaves, you could do whatever you wanted ... do you agree?"

Yes, they did. Did they understand that slavery was not freedom? Not yet.

"Jesus invites you to give your life to God, and let him teach you what He created you to be. But it's your choice; He made us with free will -- we get to choose -- and does not violate that. He made us to rule the universe with Him, as his children, as his household. But you get to choose."

"Where did you come from?" asked Ann. "How did you get here, and why are you here?"

"What year is this? I'm sorry, I don't know."

"It's the year four hundred and seventy-four, of course."

They changed the calendar. Of course.

"Do you know what year it was before they started counting over?"

People looked at each other and whispered together.

Pat spoke up. "My great grandmother said her grandmother had been born in "twenty-one fifteen," but we never knew what that meant. Do you?"

"Yes, but you won't believe me. I was born in nineteen seventy eight, over 100 years before that; and the year — nineteen seventy-eight — meant it had been almost two thousand years since Jesus was born, was killed, and was brought back to life. Somewhere after I died, they started counting over again, since they wanted to erase all knowledge of Jesus from the earth."

"After you died?"

Frank was sure, by this point, I was a lunatic.

"I was in the army you saw coming with Jesus. After the battle, and His wedding, He sent me here to help you restore your city, and others besides. He sent others like me to other cities."

"You are crazy! Come on, let's throw him off this stage!"

He lunged towards me, his left arm hanging limp by his side. I slipped out of their sight, and went back to sit next to JJ.

"I think this is going very well," I whispered to him. "What do you think?"

"I'm loving it," he said, and then jumped up, astonished.

"How did you get here?"

"Oh, sorry to have startled you." I stood up and walked back to the stage, where the Talkers where excitedly milling around looking for me.

"Frank."

He stopped, turned, and stared.

"Would you like to ask Jesus to heal that arm?"

His expression changed from anger, to surprise, to anger, to hope, and back to anger.

"Don't mess with me, you wacko. Get out of here."

"If you would like to ask, I'm sure He would do it."

"Shut up!"

"He would do it right here, right now."

Two or three others came up behind Frank, pulled on his shirt and the other arm, and said, "Do it, Frank. Do it."

I walked up onto the stage and waited.

"No!" he shouted. "Throw him off the stage!"

I looked at the others and said, "Perhaps that will help. Please come throw me off the stage. Really."

Several of the men came and gingerly took hold of me. As they began pushing, they began straining, and were obviously sweating with the effort.

"Don't hurt yourselves, please. Perhaps you need more help."

They waved at others, and then at friends in the crowd. By the time they gave up, thirty or more men were pushing hard, and I had not moved at all.

Frank watched it all, and his expression slowly changed.

When the others gave up and sat down, I stood alone, facing Frank.

"He loves you, Frank. He's called you to be a leader, a shepherd of His people. He would like to heal you. May I?"

After a long pause, Frank nodded. I walked over to him, put a hand on his bad shoulder, and said, "Thank you, Father. I ask your healing for Frank."

I stepped back and waited.

His eyes began moving around, as a person who's attention is totally turned inward. His left arm slowly came up, and higher up, until it was straight up over his head. Then he held it out to the side, did the same with his other arm, and began turning slowly in circles. Those around us began clapping, laughing, and cheering, and the clapping began a rhythm. Frank began to dance, and soon others had joined with him to form a dancing circle around the platform.

I sat down next to JJ again.

"So, now what do you think?

"I like it," he said. "I really like it."

Finally Frank collapsed into a chair and looked at me. "All right, young man. I thank you. And I apologize for ... what I've done. Suppose you get up here and tell us why you're here."

I walked up to the stage, and looked around the crowd around us. All were silent.

"The God who made us all, and paid the price to bring us into his family, finally put an end to those who refused Him, who absolutely rejected Him. He rules the Universe ... He made it ... and if you reject Him, there's no place left for you. So He waited for thousands of years, and finally brought the armies of His enemies together into one place and destroyed them."

"And all the disasters before that? The mountains collapsing, the sun going dark, the blood in the water?"

"Demonstrating his power, for any who might be convinced. Awful things, but you had believed those deceivers, so He raised the stakes far above their little tricks. He was still waiting for repentance."

There was silence for a while.

"And now?" said HL. "What happens now?"

"I assume all government is gone, all communications gone, and you have some farms, and I see a little bit of electricity being generated from somewhere. No cars, no planes ... water pipes still working, somehow?"

"Mostly," said HL. "But seriously — what happens now? Why are you here?"

"Think of it this way," I said. "Jesus is the King. Of everything. I expect Him to come here sometimes, but He makes his own plans. He sent me to help you put things back together, and to lead you to know Him and ... well, to decide."

"Decide what?"

"If you will give your life to Him ... each of you ... or not."

"Are you supposed to tell us what to do?"

"That's how the devil works. Tyranny. That's not how God works. He will guide you, each of you, and you will choose. Free will - you have it, and He respects it. He gave it to you, when He created you. I can help you hear Him, help you know Him, but He's the King. I'm not."

"What if some people don't ... behave ... don't do right. Whatever that is."

"Then I'll deal with it."

"You will."

"Yes. I will."

"How?"

I thought about that. How, indeed? How does a servant leader, a shepherd, deal with a recalcitrant sheep, on behalf of the one who owns the flock? What does it mean now, in this time and place, to "complete the suffering of Christ"? Somehow I suspected that was still going on, until the final events unfold a thousand years or more from now.

"I'll ask Him what to do, in each situation, just as you need to do."

"Sounds like chaos, to me," said Frank. "No laws?"

"If we need laws, we'll make them. But He wants relationship with you as family, not obedience from servants."

"How do we start?" asked Ann. "It's been a long day already."

"Can we meet here tomorrow?" I asked. "I don't know what you normally do, or what else you need to do."

"We need to go tell our people what we can about all this," said Ann.

"And decide if we believe it!" added Frank.

"That will come with time," I said, "and with knowing Him. Let's meet again in 7 days, and between now and then I'll move around in the city and get to know you better."

The Talkers milled around a bit, talking among themselves, and then one by one left the stage and began walking away from the park with small groups of people around them. I stood on the platform, waiting to see if any of the people would approach without the Talkers present, but none did.

JJ and his friends waited, and I walked back down to join them.

"Coming back with us?" he asked.

"Thanks, my friend, but I think I'll wander the city, as I said, and get acquainted. If you need me, just ask God to send me."

"How do we do that ... exactly?" he smiled. "Is that a magic trick?"

"Well, you need to make a decision. Here's the deal. Your rebellion, your selfishness, your hurting others, all that created a distance between you and God, who is completely good. Punishment was needed. He sent Jesus to be tortured and killed in your place. Now the debt is paid, and He wants you to come back, like a ..."

"Like a prodigal son?"

"Exactly! How do you know that story? I thought the deceivers had destroyed all the Bibles ... all the books about God."

"The books are gone," said Steve, standing quietly behind JJ. "But some people remember, and tell the stories."

I nodded. Good. There was some reference to make, some connection to what they already knew... at least for a few.

"So God is our Father, and wants his children back. Will you come?"

"How can you say he's 'good', after all He's done?"

"How could I say He's 'good,' if He never dealt with evil and just left it to fester and destroy forever?"

JJ nodded. "OK, maybe I see that ... what do I do?"

I put my hand on his head. "Father, I bring JJ to you, and ask that you make yourself known to him. Holy Spirit, please fill him with your presence, and teach him to know the voice of the King."

I stepped back. "From now on, you'll be learning to recognize His voice. Be listening — not with your physical ears, but in your mind and heart. Things will be different. And I'll see you soon."

I turned and walked around the platform to follow one of the departing groups, and I heard JJ singing. As they walked away, I heard Tank say, "I never heard you do that, not ever. You know how to sing?"

Ann

The group I was following turned out to be Ann's, from the northeast side. Farms, she had said.

When they saw me coming along behind, they stopped, and Ann came back toward me.

"Are you following us?"

"I want to get to know the people here. May I walk with you?"

"Do you have a place to stay?"

"No... don't really need one, actually."

"Why not?"

"Shall we walk?"

She turned, and we began catching up with the others who were waiting.

"I don't need to sleep, and though I enjoy eating, I don't particularly need to..."

"Why not? That's crazy. And what was that about you were born hundreds of years ago, and died already?"

"You may know some of it already. You do know the name 'Jesus,' right?"

"Sure. Mythology, like Noah, Thor, Zeus, Atlas ..."

"What do you remember about Him?"

We were walking in the middle of her group now, perhaps twenty or so, and all listening quietly.

"Prophet, did miracles, good teacher. Not much."

"Was there a time when suddenly everyone who believed in Him, who was committed to him, disappeared?"

"That's what people say. Called themselves 'Christians'? Suddenly gone. But who knows? Long time ago, and they've burned all the books, so there's no way to find out."

"The deceivers?"

"Yeah, if that's what you want to call them. Said they would tell us anything we needed to know, and burned everything."

"I can tell you what's true, and you'll have to decide whether to believe it."

"Sounds like normal life, to me!" laughed Ann. "Go ahead."

The sun was touching down to our left as I finished. Creation to resurrection to Armageddon, trumpets and bowls and wedding feast, all of it. No one spoke.

We left the main city behind as we walked, and came to a dry fountain in a small village. Ann sat down on a bench, one of many that circled the fountain.

"From here, people go different ways," she said. "What will you do tonight?"

"This is a nice place. Probably a great view of the stars, right? I might just stay here. What will you be doing tomorrow?"

"The moon will rise in a couple of hours and you won't see the stars very well after that," she said, looking at the eastern sky. "I have to go feed my family, but I'd like to come back and talk a bit after that. Be OK?"

As the moon cleared the horizon two hours later, Ann returned to the fountain with a broad-shouldered man beside her. We sat down together, looking at the fountain.

"It's running," she exclaimed. "Did you do that?"

I nodded. "What's the use of a dry fountain?"

"It's been dry for years," said the man. "Aaron's the name. You're James?" I nodded. "I'm her husband."

"How did you escape the war?" I asked.

"Broken leg," he said. "Farming accident. Couldn't walk, couldn't even stand. Not much use to an army!"

"Healed all right?"

"Yes, thanks. Doing fine, and very glad to still be here."

I smiled. I liked this young man.

"Ann's told me a lot, I'm sure not nearly all. What do you plan to do?"

"Depends on the people, I think. Not too sure. Just got this job, you might say!"

"And what job is it, exactly?"

"Jesus is the King. Heaven, earth, all of it. And as part of his Bride, as the old writings called us, those who believed in Him and stayed true through all the troubles, are now on the throne with Him, so to speak. Co-rulers, under His authority."

I paused. How to say this?

"But He is a lover-king, not a tyrant-king. Created us all to be ... family. Intimate. Loved, and returning that love. So there's an invitation on the table ... and what I do, what I need to do, depends very much on how you respond. How each person here responds."

"You don't eat? You don't sleep? Did I understand that right?"

"I'm in the body I'll have forever, like the one you'll have after you physically die. I just got there before you."

"How is it different? You look ...normal. But Ann said you did some strange things, back there. And healed Frank?"

"God did, actually. I just asked. And the main difference is that this body..." I patted my stomach. "Doesn't wear out, doesn't grow old. Doesn't get hungry or tired. I can see the angels with these eyes, and hear things ... hard to explain. Just the next phase of life. After Jesus was killed and came back, he spent 40 days visiting with his friends and followers, and I'm sure they had all the same questions. He would appear and disappear, whatever, but it was still really Him, with a real body. Ate fish with them to prove they weren't just seeing a ghost or something."

"You can see angels? They are real?"

"They are. Arul is with me tonight, sitting on that bench across the fountain. Can you tell he's there?"

Aaron stood up and looked around. "No."

"There's a lot going on in the universe that we just can't see in our original bodies. You're in the initial part of your life, but you're really just at the beginning. It's a choosing time, and a training time."

"You may not need sleep, James, but I do," yawned Ann. "Lot to do tomorrow. Farming never stops. You coming, Aaron, or you want to talk a while."

"I'll be in after a while. You go ahead."

Ann slipped away into the night, and Aaron watched the moon for a minute.

"So what's the choice you keep talking about, that we need to make?"

"To accept His love, and begin your relationship with Him... give your life to Him... or reject Him, and be ruled as a subject instead of being part of the family."

"What does that mean, to give my life to him? I have a family, I have promises to keep."

"Seems like all that just proves he loves you. Best I can tell, Ann is one of the gifts he's already given you. Agree?"

"Maybe so," said Aaron, "and I just never knew who to thank."

After a while, he said, "So would I be able to hear him? See him? See angels? What kind of a relationship can you have with someone you can't see or hear?"

"When we accept His offer, He sends His spirit, the Holy Spirit is what we learned to call Him, who knits you together with Him... and you start learning to know His voice. His whispers in your soul, His urges in your heart ... it's an intimate conversation, different for each person. He told his first followers that this Spirit was a comforter, a counselor, and would lead them into all truth. And He still does."

"Deep stuff, James. Deep stuff. I think I'll head on to bed, before I fall off this bench. Long day already, and a long one tomorrow."

He stood. "Can I get you anything? You're welcome to come to our place, of course, most welcome."

I raised a hand in farewell. "You go on. We'll meet again."

As he walked away, Arul came over. "Shall we go Home for a bit?"

HL

When we returned, I walked into the east side of the city until I came to the tracks HL had mentioned.

A group of men were sitting on the sidewalk in the morning sun, and I asked where I might find HL. One of them pointed down the street, but none of them spoke.

A cafe at the corner seemed to be the place they were sending me to, and I found HL working on some fried eggs and toast with a group gathered around him at the scattered tables.

"Just talking about you," he said, as I walked in. "Come have a seat, let these people get a good look at the newcomer!"

I waved and took a seat near HL.

"What brings you to our part of town?"

"You," I said. "Wanted a chance to get to know you."

I looked around.

"Seems like everyone's gotten shy," I said. "Hardly anyone ever speaks to me. Why is that?"

"Sorry about that," he said. He looked at various ones in the room. "We need to get over that."

"They're gone," he said to the group around us. "No need to be afraid anymore, no need to be so careful about saying what we think."

Several nodded, but no one spoke. He laughed. "See how hard it is?"

"But you're right, HL. You are." An older lady by the door spoke up. "We let them bully us, and we need to ... to come out of that!"

He nodded. "Everyone else agree? No need to be cowed by people who aren't even here any more!"

He looked at me for confirmation. "And won't be coming back, you said?"

"That's right, HL. They are gone."

A wave of relief seemed to move through the room, and people were noticeably more relaxed.

"Want something to eat?" he asked.

"What's the best thing on the menu?" I asked. "Never been here before!"

"Charlie, what do you think? Sam? Jeanne?"

The consensus was that I should try the Reuben sandwich, if I liked that sort of thing. Didn't take long to become a fan.

"I'll need to remember where I am!" I said. "What do you call this place?"

"Kim's. Just Kim's. That's it."

The lady who had brought the sandwich waved from the kitchen counter, and I waved back. "Excellent. Thank you!"

"How much do I owe her?" I asked HL.

He looked at me for a moment, as though trying to decide how to answer. "That's a good question. They took away our money... back when the tattoos and all were done... and we didn't pay for anything. Now that they're gone ... how will it work?"

He pointed to Kim in the kitchen. "She does things for us, like that sandwich. Like my eggs." He mopped up the last of the yolk with his toast. "And we do things for her, like the table you're sitting at ... I put that back together last week."

"So there's no financial system left."

"Nope," he agreed. "Told you I was a lawyer. There's no law, no law enforcement, no jails. No money, no banks. There's just all of us, living together, trying to decide how we'll go on."

Someone spoke up. Charlie?

"Are you a leader of some kind? What are you here for? HL told us some interesting things you did, and said."

"The King has sent me to help. What that means depends on what you need, I suppose."

"The King? We don't have a king. Had ... whatever they were ... and before that we elected people, but no kings. Not here."

"He's what every other king should have been, Charlie, and what we all wished a king would be through the centuries. You'll see when you meet him. In the meanwhile, I'll do what I can."

"Like what? What will you do?"

"HL, what's the most pressing need here?"

"Water. Sanitation. Electricity, next - for those who have light bulbs and things that run on it. You do know, the world was shaken pretty badly?"

"I do," I said, and decided to leave it at that.

"So the pipes and such underground are pretty much useless. This town was built on a river, so we can work things out as far as getting water to everyone; some towns weren't, so I suppose they are empty by now."

"You must have farms all around."

"First thing to be put back together, since people need food. Pretty good system for bringing food into the town."

"You said there were no laws, no law enforcement. Is everyone doing what's right? Anyone causing trouble?

"I would have said Frank was a concern, until you did whatever you did! He's a changed man."

Two or three spoke up then, asking about Frank and what had happened. HL explained.

Jeanne spoke up, but still only speaking to HL. "Could he come to my house? Dan is ... in pretty bad shape."

HL looked at me. "Maybe you should ask him."

New Gifts

Jeanne turned to me, and it seemed to be a great effort to speak. "My husband is dying."

That's all she said, but the Spirit instantly urged me forward. I stood up. "May I come with you?"

The entire room was on its feet in a heartbeat.

No one spoke, but everyone clearly felt invited. They waited for me to follow Jeanne out the door, and then silently trailed along. We walked four blocks, turned down a side street — Abram, I noticed — and another six blocks. No one else was around; it was as though the entire population of the neighborhood had been at Kim's, and was now going to be in Jeanne's living room.

She turned into a gated yard, and we walked up a long sidewalk to the front door steps.

The entire group moved easily into the living room of Jeanne's home, and we found Dan on a couch under a front window, holding a washcloth over his face. He looked up and hardly expressed any emotion as we trooped in.

"Sorry I couldn't come," he whispered. "Nice of you to bring the meeting here!"

"Dan, this is James," said Jeanne, and no more.

He looked at me silently for a moment, and then said, "Welcome to our home, James. Forgive me for not getting up."

Then he began coughing, and it went on for a minute or two before he could get his breath. He spoke no more, but simply looked at me, and seemed to be concentrating on breathing slowly and calmly.

"Can you help him?" asked Jeanne, quietly.

"Father can," I said. "Let's ask Him."

I looked around at those who had come, and said, "The God who made you loves you. He's cleared away the barriers between us and Him, and He invites you to know Him. He's given all authority to Jesus, the King, and that's who sent me here... to tell you about Him, and invite you into the family."

I kneeled down in front of Dan, and said, "May I ask Him to heal you?"

In a pale, almost inaudible voice, he said, "Please."

I put a hand on his chest. "Father, I thank you that you hear me, and I know that you always hear me. I thank you for these who have come, and for sending me to Dan. Now I ask for your healing for him, and ... please make yourself known to him. Let him hear your voice, and know it's You."

Dan closed his eyes and seemed to almost stop breathing. We waited in that quiet room, and there was only the sound of feet shuffling now and then, and an occasional cough. I waited like everyone else, knowing that there was nothing else to be done but wait on the One who could do what we asked.

After several minutes, a lady's quiet voice behind me began singing. Not a voice I recognized, and then I noticed it was not a language I recognized, either. A deeper voice began humming along, and then began a different song. A different language. Again, not one I recognized, but I began to smile.

Another, and another, and another joined in, and as I looked around, I saw a number of faces that were no longer focused on what was happening with Dan, but on what was happening inside. Inside their own hearts and minds.

I watched as each one began to light up, to smile, to hum or sing or even laugh, and the room steadily filled with the cascading music and laughter that is not from this earth. Several minutes went by, and it then settled down into a quieter harmony, and then ceased.

I looked back at Dan. He was sitting up, hands raised high, and face glowing as he looked upward.

"Thank you, Jesus", I said, "for sending Your Spirit, and letting me see it begin. We love you."

"Jeanne, may we invite everyone to sit down? I think there may be some questions!"

"Please," she said, "please, everyone, make yourselves comfortable. Jesse, Bill, Tommy, there are more chairs in that room, could you bring them?"

With everyone settled, I looked around.

"What has He said to you?"

"Those thoughts in my head, those words that seemed to be someone speaking to me ... and pictures ... was that Him?" asked Dan, and I could tell from his face that it was.

"Tell us what He said, if you can."

"There was a picture of this city, full of life again, but a healthy life, a clean life, not driven by monsters. And I saw myself in a room at a table, with others, and a huge ... auditorium ... of people watching us. And there was a door that opened, and a man came in ... glowing ... in a robe that seemed to be stained around the bottom, and he had a crown."

He stopped, and looked intently at me. "That was Jesus, wasn't it? Somehow I know... that was Him."

I nodded. "Anyone else?" I asked. "Don't worry if it does not seem to fit what Dan saw... it will always be different, as He gives each of us a piece of the puzzle, a piece of the whole picture."

A young woman raised her hand, and as she spoke, I recognized that she had been the first to start singing.

"Rebecca. Thank you, Mr. James, for healing my father, and for ... whatever just happened. Can you tell us what that was, what just happened to us?"

"Think of God expressing himself in three ways," I said. "The Father, who is the creator, the source of all we see, but invisible to human eyes; His son, Jesus, who is the full expression of the Father — the "Word of God" is one of His names — who became one of us as well, to bridge the gap; and then the Spirit, the power, the one He sends to live with us, to join with our spirits... to fill us, as some call it. And that's who you just met... the Spirit of God."

"Will He leave?"

"No, I think not," I smiled. "It is said that 'the gifts and call of God are irrevocable," and the gift of his own spirit to live inside us is one of those gifts!"

There was silence for a while, and someone began speaking in one of those new languages. Suddenly they stopped, and looked around. It was HL, and he had a confused look.

"What was that?" he said.

"A new language. Use it whenever you want. It's private, just between your spirit and God."

"So I was talking to God just then? What was I saying?"

"I don't know," I said, but maybe someone here will suddenly hear words in their head and can tell us. Or maybe it was His Spirit in you talking to the Father, expressing things you are unable to express or understand."

"HL," said Dan, in a voice much stronger than I had heard him use before, "you were praying for this city. I understood you!"

HL shook his head. "Very strange, that's what I think. Very strange! But you're well, Dan? Are you well?"

Dan slowly stood up, stretched to his full height, and spread his arms out wide. "I feel great!" he said. He took a long, slow, deep breath, and then sat back down. "Weak, for sure, but I feel ... well. I think I'm well. Thank you, young man, thank you."

I bowed a little, and then laughed. "All I did was ask. You heard me! And each of you ..." I turned around, pointing at each person in the room, "each of you can do the same. He loves you just as He loves me, no difference. So get to know the Spirit that has come to live in you. Learn His voice, and let

Him teach you how to live this new life! And now I think I should leave, and let you talk as friends, and share the gift."

I bowed slightly to Jeanne, and we shared a smile. Then I stepped out to the front porch, and left in the Spirit.

The Good Times

Immediately I found myself walking along a road out in the country with only farmlands in every direction. One farm was growing a good crop, and three more were overgrown with brush and weeds, and then another one was well maintained. Lack of people, lack of resources. But much opportunity to rebuild and refresh themselves, with God's blessing.

A horse approached from behind, and then another. As I stepped to the side of the road they galloped by, and the first rider shouted, "Get aside, you!" The second one added his embellishment.

They were 50 feet past me when I spoke. "Come back," I said quietly to the horses. They pulled up suddenly, and somehow the riders stayed on as they turned and began trotting back to me.

"Stop it! Whoa! What are you doing, you stupid animal?"

Their cries and complaints were to no avail, and the horses came back to stand before me.

"Thank you," I said. "Blessings. Are these gentlemen being rough on you?" The paint vigorously nodded and neighed, and the roan gently agreed. "Should they walk instead? Would you rather go free of them?"

I sensed that was exactly what they would prefer, and I was agreeable to it. "Get down," I said to the riders. They stared at me. "You can forget that!" said the tall blond man, roughly and with a coarse laugh. "Ain't happening!"

"Arul, would you do the favors?"

The blond man suddenly rose from the saddle and flew sideways, landing in the brush and gravel past the side of the road.

"And you?" I said to the other, a smaller young man with dirty hair, dirty clothes, and a sour look. He seemed frozen for a moment, still looking at his friend, then scrambled to get off the roan.

"Thank you."

Then I turned back to the horses. "Now you two are free to go, but come back home by evening, because they are charged with your care."

The horses neighed, turned, and trotted off. A few yards away they turned into a field and were quickly out of site, running free.

I spoke to the younger man, as his friend struggled to climb out of the weeds.

"James," I said. "Your name?"

"Sid," he said. "And that's Simeon."

"Hello, Simeon, are you OK?"

Simeon stepped up onto the road, glaring at me. "Who the blazes are you, and how did you do that?"

"The name is James. I just asked the horses to bring you back to me, and they did. You were mistreating them, and me too, for that matter."

"They're mine. I own them! I can do whatever I want to them!"

"They belong to God, who created them, just as He created you. Did you know there are horses in heaven?"

"Sid, this man is wacky. We need to teach him some manners!"

Sid shook his head. "Simeon. Listen to me. He just threw you off the horse, without even touching you! Don't be stupid!"

Simeon came up close to me, furious, fists clenched.

I smiled at him. "Go ahead, my friend. I don't mind."

That was all the encouragement he needed. He drew back and hit me as hard as a sledgehammer, with muscles trained by daily work in the field. He threw his whole body at me, led by his fist. I didn't actually see Arul do this, but I knew he put his hand in front of my face just at that moment. I heard several bones in that hand crack, and Simeon fell to his knees clutching that hand with his other one.

I turned to his friend. "Sid, where do you live?"

Staring at Simeon, he motioned down the road in the direction they had been going. "A mile or so ..."

"I'm going to spend the night at your house. Let's start walking, and perhaps Simeon will come along when he's ready."

Sid slowly turned to walk with me.

"Farmers?" I asked.

He nodded. "Trying to keep things going."

He turned his head back towards Simeon. "He's been angry ever since the war. We couldn't go, and no one else came back. It's been hard."

I nodded. No doubt about that.

"Brothers? No, just friends, I think. Farms next to one another, so you grew up together. And the horses are yours, not his ... regardless of what he said."

Sid stopped in the road. "How do you know that?"

"There's a God in heaven who loves you, both of you, and sent me to introduce you to him. He told me."

"You really are wacky," said Sid. "For real."

By the time we turned in to the house they shared and sat down on the porch, Simeon was coming along the road, still clutching his hand

He scowled and cursed at me as he came up the path to the porch steps. "Get out of here!"

"Would you like that to be fixed?"

"I'd like you to be gone, that's what I'd like!"

"We can ask God to put your hand back together."

"And you can ask Him to give us some rain, while you're at it!" he retorted.

A light sprinkle began, as a cloud moved over us from behind the house. Simeon stared up at it. I laughed, and said to Sid, "I love it when He does that."

Sid just shook his head, looking up at the cloud. It was getting quickly darker, and the drops were getting bigger.

"Come have a seat, Simeon, and give up being angry. You were a happy man before the war, and you can be that again."

"You did not know me, and this rain has nothing to do with you."

A thunderclap made them both jump, and Simeon quickly ran up the steps. Rain poured heavily around us.

"Let's see, we were talking about asking God to heal your hand ... which would be as crazy as asking Him for rain, wasn't that your thought?"

He held up his hand, blue and swollen and obviously in great pain. "This? Where you hit me? You're gonna pray and this is gonna be fixed?"

"Only if you want me to. God lets us choose, and right now, you're making some pretty bad choices. This could be a great chance to change your pattern!"

"Fine," shouted Simeon. "Ask Him! Fix it, if you can."

As he held his hand up before us, the color changed, the swelling disappeared, and the look on his face was everything you would expect. Sid and I both laughed, and then looked at each other, and laughed again.

Simeon stared at his hand, flexing his fingers. Then he stared at me.

"Sit down, Simeon. Enjoy the rain, and let's talk."

Turned out Simeon had had a pretty rough time of it. He was a good young man, turned bitter by too many frustrations, too many defeats, too many seasons with not enough rain and not enough crop, too much 'too much' to recover from, or even endure.

"You did not go to the battle?"

"Too sick. Fever. Almost died." He stood up, went to the door, and disappeared inside.

Sid held up a hand to say, "Wait."

I watched the rain clouds dissipate and drift away, and the sun came back out to dry up the grass and the dirt road.

Simeon returned with a tray and glasses full of a cold cider. Cool, anyway.

"Thank you, Simeon!" I said. "I think your hand is feeling better!"

He nodded. "I don't understand any of this, you know that, right?"

"Sure," I said. "Enemy aliens come out of the sky and kill everyone, then it turns out it was God, and I show up to say He loves you. It would make anyone's head spin."

"But it's true?"

"Look at your hand."

He did, and shook his head. "Was that really your face that I hit, and my hand broke?"

"Actually, no. There's an angel with me. He put up a hand to protect me, and you ... well, swinging at an angel is a poor idea."

He laughed. "I'll sure try to remember that next time!"

"I looked at Arul, standing in the yard, and he was smiling.

"He thinks it's funny too, seems like."

"Can you see him?"

"Sure, right there." I pointed.

"Can other people?"

"Sometimes, when he wants them to. But as far as I know, you're the only one who's ever touched him!"

Arul laughed at that, and nodded.

"Well, I sure did that." He looked out into the yard. "Sorry, sir."

Arul waved an acknowledgement.

"You're just one step away from being able to see lots of things, and start being the man God created you to be."

"All right," said Sid. "You've been hinting at that. What's the deal?"

"His life for yours. The debt has been paid. Will you accept the deal?"

"Well, you make it sound pretty simple. Any details around that?"

"It's an exchange," I explained. "Give Him your life, and He credits you with the payment He made on the cross. Paid in full. Now you live for Him."

"What's the alternative?"

"Go on messing up your life on your own, and eventually have to make the same choice, but without the good times in between. And in the end, the very end, there's no place in the universe for those who refuse Him. Oh, and in about a thousand years, Satan is coming back for one last sweep ... to gather up everyone he can, in a final rebellion."

We sat for a while watching the afternoon sun drift down.

"What do you mean, 'the good times?'" asked Sid.

I smiled, remembering some times in my own life I would not have called 'good' in the moment.

"He wants you to be a shepherd, helping take care of His sheep ... His people. Which is really everyone. Some sheep are rebellious, mean, untrustworthy, and some are great. There are wolves and bears to deal with. You will be criticized and hated. The weather can be bad, and the sheep never say 'thank you' for anything. You protect them, you do what you can to heal their wounds, you make mistakes, you get bruised. Maybe you get killed, like He did. You know, normal shepherd stuff. Good times."

"Sorry," said Sid. "I missed it. Where in that list was the 'good times' part?"

"Belonging to Him."

"And the 'one step' you mentioned?" asked Simeon. "That's when you take the deal?"

I nodded.

"And ... how would I take the deal, if I were foolish enough to sign up?"

"Just tell Him. He's always waiting for those words!"

"He can hear me, like right here? Right now?"

"All the time."

"OK, God!" he shouted. "It's a deal! Probably crazy, but no worse than where I am now, and you're not getting much in the trade."

The sound echoed back from inside the house, and faded into the distance down the road.

Simeon leaned back with his eyes closed. Suddenly he sat straight up.

"Your angel."

"Yes?"

"He's right there, isn't he? By the gate?"

"Yes, exactly."

"Ask him to move."

"You ask him. His name is Arul."

He hesitated. "Not used to talking to invisible people ... Arul! Would you mind, please, sir, moving one way or the other? I just want to know ... I really do almost see you, I think!"

Arul stepped out onto the road and walked back the way we had come.

"Hey, you don't have to leave ..." and Simeon's voice trailed off.

I laughed. "Sounds like you saw him just fine!"

"He just walked that way, down the road, didn't he?"

"Yup."

"This is crazy. Sid, did you see him?"

We turned to look at Sid, and he was leaning back in the rickety old chair with his eyes closed and his hands in his lap, palms up, as though someone were going to place something in them.

Looks good, I thought. Looks very good.

What About Money?

At the next meeting of the Talkers, I was welcomed by several, and looked at with increased interest by those I had not yet met.

"Still here?" asked one, a burly fellow with a friendly face and a red bush of a beard. "Thought you would have been bored and gone by now!"

"Go ahead," I laughed. "Bore me! May be harder than you think!"

"Today," said Frank, starting the meeting, "we need to decide about money."

"Like what to use, and what it's worth?" asked Ann.

"And how we make it and control it, all that stuff."

"Do you need it?" I asked.

Frank looked at me with his mouth open in mid-sentence. Finally he slowly answered me, as though speaking to a deaf child. "Of course we need it. Every society needs it. Otherwise we'll be trading corn for shoes and pigs for ... sewing work. Whatever we need."

"And the problem with that is ...?" I asked.

"What if the person with pigs needs sewing work, but the one who can sew doesn't want pigs ... wants corn, actually?"

"It's a good question," I answered. "What if the person who could sew offered to sew for the person with pigs, and the person with corn offered some to the person who was hungry?

And we took care of each other, and we did not invent bureaucracy and tough problems to manage?"

There was silence for a minute. Some of them thought that was actually a pretty good idea, and others thought anyone who would suggest that was a naïve fool. I could read it on everyone's faces.

Ann seemed to like the idea. "Ann," I said, "you take the ball on this. Figure out how that would work, how it could work, and come back to describe it next time."

Frank stood looking at me again, as though a child had just stolen a basketball from him as he started to dribble down the court. "Wait a minute," he finally said. "Who are you to tell Ann what to do, and to interrupt our talking it over?"

I just watched Ann and waited. When she quietly said, "OK," it was over. The subject changed, and Frank could not believe it.

Samuel

JJ came up to me after the meeting.

"Remember that place I told you not to go?"

I nodded.

"Maybe you should go there."

"Why?"

"It feels like a spider nest, somehow ... creepy ... every time we walk past it, I can feel the place. It's bad."

"Did you notice that feeling before...?"

"No, man, just since you put your hand on me, remember?"

"So here's what's happening. You've got some new antenna. You're being aware of more things, things you were blind to before. You're probably aware of where Arul is, if you want to notice."

"Really? Like, right now, I could almost see him?"

"Sure. Where do you think he is?"

JJ closed his eyes, then opened them and looked around. "There. Right there. Under that big branch."

Arul waved at us. I laughed. "He's waving at you, and you're exactly right."

"Wow," said JJ. "Wow."

"So you can tell the place is bad news, huh?"

"Been rumors, you know, like people went in there and never came out. But now, it's like, I can feel the creepiness oozing out around the door when I walk by!"

"Anyone else feel it?"

"Nah, I checked. Nobody else."

"I'll walk back that far with you, and we'll see what's going on." He nodded, and waved at the others. "Ready?"

"Waitin' on you, man, just waitin' on you," said Tank, and the group began moving.

We came to the shop he had told me about.

"You guys go on.."

JJ and I stopped in front of the store. It seemed open, but for what? No particular kind of business was promoted by the signs.

"You said this is one of the Talkers?"

"Samuel, I think. Not sure who he represents... maybe no one. He was there in a red shirt today, did not say anything at all... Just watched you, mainly, I think."

There was a darkness inside that was more than the absence of light. I looked at Arul, and he rose up over the building, taking a position of shielding it, isolating it.

I took the handle of the door and tried to sense what was inside, but it just felt cold. Spiritually cold, not physically.

We pushed it open and walked inside. No one was at the counter, and nothing stirred in the rooms beyond it.

"Hello?" I called.

A chair creaked in the back. A man in a red shirt came into the hallway and walked slowly to the counter. He came to us, put both hands on the counter, and said nothing. He just looked briefly at JJ, nodded, and then looked at me and waited.

"My name is James. Yours?"

He did not answer, and his expression did not change. He was a big man, strong, but there was a deadness in his face, a look that was beyond despair, the empty eyes of someone who had arrived at a complete loss of hope.

"You have electricity," I observed. "Seems to me that few buildings have that, and that no way exists today to buy it... how does that work?"

He cocked his head, as though trying to discern the reason behind my asking, or my visit for that matter.

"I asked for it. Jemsen has that part of the city, where the generators are, and he turned it on for me."

Nothing else. Not a talkative guy, apparently.

"Do others simply have to ask, and it will be provided? Does Jemsen ask something in return?"

"Don't know."

"Did he ask anything in return, from you?"

"No."

Another silence.

I was suddenly aware of another presence down the hall, a spirit that was biding its time, staying out of sight. I spoke to it.

"Come out."

Samuel started back, put his hands up, and said, "What are you doing?" His eyes grew wide, and he seemed to be trembling. He backed up until he stood with his shoulders against the wall behind him.

I held a hand up to him, to say "wait." He did not move or speak.

Again I spoke to the thing down the hall.

"Come out now."

A door opened, and a greenish light spilled into the hallway. It darkened as a large creature in the shape of a man bent down to get under the door frame and emerge. It was fully 8 feet tall and not exactly human. It straightened up and lumbered slowly towards us. JJ backed up, and Samuel slid down the wall away from the hallway.

"What ... do you want, James? I know Who sent you."

Its voice was deep, raspy, and painful to listen to. I noticed an unusual number of fingers as it pointed a hand to me to ask the question.

"You need to leave," I said. "Your masters are dead, Lucifer is imprisoned, and your kind are not welcome here any more."

"Leave? And go where, little man? Where would you send me?"

I put the question before the Spirit, and waited for the answer. "It appears you have a choice," I told him. "You may go into the abyss with Lucifer, or into outer darkness."

"I choose neither! And you cannot make me!"

The creature stormed back down the hall, ducked under the doorframe, and slammed the door closed behind him.

"Arul?" I said. He was suddenly with us in the room, and JJ jumped out of his way. I laughed. "So you see him, JJ?"

"Almost! I sure know he's here!"

"Who? What? What's happening?" asked Samuel, now trembling visibly.

"Arul, you heard the conversation, I'm sure. Are you able to take this creature away?"

"My pleasure." With that, Arul walked straight forward through the counter and through the wall of the first office. A moment later there was a scream that began loudly but quickly faded, as though moving to a great distance, and then was gone.

The atmosphere immediately brightened, and seemed even physically lighter, as though every molecule of air had been carrying a weight of grey shroud and was now set free.

"Oh!" exclaimed Samuel, as he fell into a swivel chair. "Oh! He's gone! I can feel it! He's gone!"

I watched him, enjoying the sight, as I always do, the delightful sight of the captives being set free.

"Samuel, do you need to tell us what he's been doing?"

He cringed at the thought.

"All right," I said. "He's gone, and that's gone. The question now is... what are you going to do?"

He sat with his head down, and finally looked up at me with a glance towards JJ. "I helped him .. I didn't want to , but he made me ..."

"Samuel, the king, the man named Jesus, has paid the price for all you've done. Will you accept that? Will you let it go, and let his payment with his own life be sufficient for your mistakes and actions?"

"Can I? Is that ... can that be really true?"

JJ was nodding excitedly and smiling.

"Of course! If I can believe it!" continued Samuel.

"Then just speak to him now ... he hears everything you say ... and tell Him you accept, and that you'll give Him your life in trade for His."

"Jesus?" He asked.

"Yes, that's his name."

He looked off in the corner of the window, and said, "Jesus, I don't know you. But if you can take the awful darkness away, and I can walk free... please do it."

He hesitated, and then added, "And I'll give you my wretched life, if you have any use for it."

He then stared intently at that spot on the wall, and a smile slowly grew on his face. He leaned back in the chair, closed his eyes, and lifted his hands.

Amazing, I thought. Such a universal, automatic reaction. It's the most natural thing in the world to do at this moment.

"JJ," I said. He looked at me, and I nodded my head towards the door. He opened it and we slipped out, and I doubt Samuel had any idea when we had left.

Electricity

"JJ, can you take me to this man that controls electricity? 'Jemsen', he said?"

"Sure. Now? Tomorrow? It will be dark soon."

I didn't care, but JJ would want to be home by dark, and probably Jemsen wouldn't want to have visitors after nightfall.

"Tomorrow's fine. Shall I come stay the night at your place?"

"Sure!" said JJ, and began walking briskly that way.

"What's your hurry?" I asked.

He stopped and looked back at me, but did not immediately answer. Then he said, "I guess it's the habit, and fear. Those men never let anyone be out after dark, and nobody had lights anyway."

"OK, thanks," I said, and we walked together at a bit slower pace.

"When will Arul be back?" JJ asked.

"He's above us now, watching the city."

JJ looked up and shook his head. "Could'a fooled me!"

The next morning I was the "new guy" again, so I cooked oatmeal a second time for the young men, and they came to the table more eagerly than they had for my first experiment.

"Tank, I think you like this!" I teased him. He looked up, did not say anything, and did not stop eating.

After breakfast we started out.

"How far?" I asked.

"Ten blocks, maybe?" suggested JJ. Dave had also come along, and he thought it was maybe even further. We were walking into the rising sun, so apparently it was due east.

"Do you know him?"

"Sure, everyone knows the Talkers. He was an engineer or somethin', crippled, couldn't go to war. Ended up the only one nearby who understood the electrical stuff."

"Dave, you seem to be someone who thinks about things."

JJ laughed. "Yeah, forever!"

"There's no money being used now, true?" He nodded. "So how should that work? Do we need to create money again, or learn some new ways of doing things for each other without that?"

"Now you've done it," said JJ. "We won't hear about anything else for a month!"

Dave smiled at him, but just said, "Let me ... think on that."

We walked in silence, and I enjoyed the warm sunshine. Except for the little bit of rain over Simeon and Sid's house, there hadn't been any rain that I remembered. I realized I had no idea what season we were in, or what climactic zone.

"Is this summer? Spring? What part of the year are we in?"

Dave stared at me. "You ... what part of the world were you in, before you got here? The other side of the equator? No, you could figure that out ... do you really not know?"

I shook my head. "I wasn't here. I just got to this world ... what has it been, three weeks now, since I showed up at your house?"

"You just got to this ... world?"

I realized our prior conversation had not soaked in.

JJ chimed in. "Dave, he explained that. You don't remember?"

"Maybe I didn't understand ... I'm sure I didn't ..."

"Sorry. But anyway... what season is this?"

"Springtime, maestro. Just beginning to get hot, and it will be blistering soon."

"Shouldn't you be having rain, then? Especially if summer is really dry?"

"Yeah, we should." JJ looked around the sky. "Now that you mention it... haven't had any for a while!"

"Are the Talkers worried about that, or has anyone mentioned it? Won't the farms have problems, if it doesn't come?"

"Sure."

"Which means food would get short."

"Yeah, I guess so. Oh, here's Jemsen's place."

An industrial building covered the north side of the block, and towers rose behind that. The towers connected to other towers in all four directions with heavy cables fairly high up.

We opened the main door into the building on this side, and found ourselves in a huge warehouse. No one was in sight.

We walked down the side aisle past stacks of electrical pipe, coils of wire, and shelves of switches, racks, tools, and boxes labeled with part numbers and "This Side Up".

At the end of the building we turned to the north and came to an office area. We opened the glass door between the offices and the warehouse and wandered in.

"Hello... hello ..." we shouted, but no answer came.

"Maybe he's out fixing a wire somewhere," suggested Dave.

Suddenly a big man was standing in front of us, waiting for us to reach him.

"Jemsen," he said. "I know you guys ... and you're the new fellow, aren't you? James?"

"Hello, Jemsen," I answered. "Yes. How are you?"

He slapped his right leg. "The old wound is giving me grief today," he said. "Sorry I couldn't come meet you further back down your trail. Better to just wait. Come on in."

He turned and limped into a large office with a conference table, two couches, an executive desk, and some swivel chairs.

He dropped into a chair at the conference table. "Have a seat, gentlemen, and talk to me."

I looked around the room, and saw no evidence that anyone else had been there in a long time. There were no used coffee cups, no notes written on the marker board, no notepads out... nothing in the trash can. Nothing on the top of the executive desk, in fact. No books on the bookshelves.

"Jemsen, it looks like no one uses this room. Do you have another place where you work on things?"

"I guess this is where they used to decide things. Paperwork. I don't do much paperwork now, so ... no paper."

He looked around.

"But we can sit here and talk. What's on your mind?"

"What's the situation with electricity?"

"We've got some generators. And we get a little fuel from our neighbors on the north, they've got some wells. But the ... can I call them dictators? The ones who are gone? They were big on pushing people around, but had no interest in things like people having electricity, or gas, or anything. So everything was crumbling even before the battle."

"How do you decide who gets power? Do you have enough for everyone?"

"Yeah, probably we do, there are so few left. But it's just me, and a little help now and then, so ..." He shrugged. "I do what I can."

"Is there a process? If someone wants to be hooked up, what do they do? And how do they pay for it?"

He scratched his balding head and yawned. "That's a good question. Two of them, I guess. Actually, three!"

He looked around the room. "Nobody here to take the request ... and almost nobody to do the work."

"If JJ here wanted some electricity for his home, what would he do?"

"Where are you?" asked Jemsen, looking at JJ.

"53 and Zenith".

"Mmm." Jemsen stared up into the corner of the ceiling. "Got anything to offer for it?"

"I could work for you," JJ said after a moment. "Got nothing else going on. Sounds like maybe you could use some workers? I can learn."

"He's good with his hands," said Dave. "And I'm good at reading things, figuring things out that way."

"Sounds like a deal," laughed Jemsen. "Let's get power to your place, so you can learn how it works. Then I can show you what's here, all the parts and supplies and such, and we can pull out the basic plans for what used to feed the city... I'll bet we can start getting things going again!"

Going North

I approached the next city from the south, on a wide, dusty asphalt road with no markings and no traffic. It looked like a fortress from a distance, and not much better up close. No sign of life.

The sun blistered the dry dirt and rocks around the city. No sign of any farming going on. How do they eat?

Behind the city a ravine branched off to the west, and the hills further back quickly became mountains. A stream wandered down from highlands on the east and flowed into the ravine.

I walked up to the gate into the city. Solid wood or metal, high and wide, it offered no visibility of what was inside. I heard no sound.

A handle of sorts waited in the middle of the door, but pulling on it did nothing. I picked up a rock the size of my fist and used it to bang on the door.

After five minutes or more, a voice called from the wall above me.

"Password?"

"The King has come," I answered.

"Nope, that ain't it. Go away."

I still had not seen anyone. I picked up the rock and banged on the door again. Immediately there was a response;

a rock flew down from the top of the wall and broke apart on the asphalt at my feet.

"What part of 'Go away' was tough to get your mind around, stranger?"

I looked up, and still saw no one. I turned to Arul.

"Shall we go in?"

Arul put both hands on the door and pushed. Fifteen feet high and perhaps twenty feet wide, it fell flat, and we walked in on top of it.

A cluster of twenty or so stared at us, and it looked like they had just scrambled to get out of the way.

"Anyone hurt under that?" I asked, pointing to the door.

"No ... " answered a white-haired man at the front of the group. "Are you going to fix what you broke?"

I looked at the door. "No, probably not. I think a little open air would do you good."

"Now, look ..." he said, gathering some courage and stepping towards me. "Don't know how you did that, but you just tore down our gate, and you need to fix it!"

A boy of ten or so peeked out from behind him and stared.

"I'm James," I said, offering my hand. He lifted his hand in a vague salute. "Patrick," he mumbled. "Not gonna fix our door?"

Looking around the entry court and on into the city streets I could see from there, I saw no one else.

"Are you the entire city?" I asked, waving at the assembled group.

Patrick stood tall, paused, and then slumped a little and said, "Yes."

"So you're afraid."

He nodded.

"I think I can help," I said. "We need to talk. Would you rather not stand out here in the sun?"

We looked at each other for half a minute or so, then he turned and talked with the people huddled behind him. A lady stepped out. "Come with me," she said, pointing down a street that ran west. The others stood and waited, so I followed her.

She led me to a small doorway into a wide room with a tall ceiling, cool and comfortable after the walk. A chair was offered, and a mug of cool water appeared. I sat down, and the others filed into the room, taking seats around the floor and in the few other chairs available.

Patrick sat at the table opposite me. He folded his hands, said nothing, and waited.

"What do you want?" I asked. "How can I help you?"

"People come up from the south and take from us," he said. "We need to close the door."

"What do they take?"

He pursed his lips, and did not want to answer. I asked the Father, and the answer poured into my mind.

"You have gems from the mountains behind you, but few people strong enough to bring in more. You have flocks in the lower hills, and strangers come to take sheep, cows, and goats from you. Since there's no money, they just take things, and maybe would still do that even if there were a way to pay you."

Patrick's mouth fell further open as I talked, until finally he realized his mouth was hanging open and closed it with an embarrassed look. "Who told you that?" he whispered.

"What do you want from God?" I asked. "He sent me to help."

"What God? The serpent the Leaders obeyed?"

"He is locked up, and he certainly was not God. You know the Leaders are gone?"

"Of course. We saw the battle."

"The one who came in the sky is Jesus, and He sent me to invite you to know Him, to belong to Him. He is God's son."

A man from the back of the group spoke, staring intently at me from under great black eyebrows. "That alien that killed our people ... he wants to help us, now? After all that?"

"The leaders rejected Him, and finally their time came. You rejected him too; I can see your tattoo is almost gone, but you took that willingly, even though people told you it was rebellion against God."

He did not speak, but finally nodded.

"But mercy triumphs over judgment, and He invites you again. The earthquakes, the mountains moving, the moon of blood and the blackened sun ..."

Mr. Eyebrows nodded, and others did too.

"Those were warnings. Showing you that the power of the Leaders was trivial, and God was in control."

"The blood and poison in the seas and rivers?"

"Yes," I said. "Trying to get your attention."

"Why didn't he just come talk to us, directly?"

"He did. They crucified Him. Perhaps you've heard the story?"

"That fable?" scoffed Eyebrows. "That legend? If that ever happened, it was too long ago to matter!"

"His patience is a mercy. Would you rather judgment had come sooner?"

"So ..." said Patrick, while Eyebrows scowled at me. "Why would we want help from such a violent, brutal God?"

"What He offers is Himself," I said quietly. "The creator of everything wants you to be in his family. And he doesn't justify himself to anyone... He is. Whether you accept Him is your choice."

"So do a miracle. Prove it." Eyebrows was standing up now, agitated.

"You saw miracles from the Leaders. What did those prove? What you need is to meet Him. He does miracles at His choosing, not mine."

"Prove it, or get out."

I waited, and the answer was clear. "Your wife was seven when you met her, Arthur. She died at twenty, just ten days after you married."

He stared at me, and the look of anger was melting into shock.

"Her grandfather never liked you, so she was alienated from her family because of you, and they've never forgiven you. Shall I remind you how she died?"

Tears began to flow. "Stop," he said.

"But God has forgiven you, and offers you peace and healing of those deep, deep wounds."

He dropped to his knees, weeping. I stood up and went to him.

"Father, thank you for Arthur, and for sending me here. I bring him to You for the healing You've offered, and I ask that he know You, and that he would introduce You to many."

More Arrive

When a new group came to the city a few days later, they had a cart piled high with clothes and sacks and tools. It was built for an ox to pull, but Samuel was with them, and he had tied the harness to a strap that ran over his shoulders and he walked along as though nothing were in that cart.

The others wore packs and carried sacks, and the group looked like refugees from war. Arthur and James met them at the gate.

"Samuel, good to see you again! Did you leave anything at home?" laughed James.

"Nothing," said Ruth, as they stopped outside the wall. "We're hoping this can be home now."

Patrick, Sarah, and the others came out and silently lined up in front of the door.

Ruth stepped up to Sarah. "I'm sorry," she said, and waved at her friends. "We have taken things from you. We've had nothing but hunger, and no money to pay anyone for anything."

Sarah nodded quietly.

"Welcome!" said Arthur. "Samuel? Is that it? You really are as strong as you look!"

Samuel ducked his head, and self-consciously put down the oxcart handles. "Hello," he mumbled. Then, with a smile, he looked up behind James and said, "I can see you now!"

Patrick looked up to follow Samuel's gaze, then nudged James. "What is he looking at?"

"He met Jesus, and apparently his eyes are a lot better now! That's our friend Arul, who put your wall back in place. He's just behind us there, on your left. Where Samuel is looking."

"Well," said Patrick, glancing up again and giving up. He turned to Ruth. "And you'd like to join us here?"

She nodded, and the others with her nodded as well. "We can help," said Samuel. "We can work. Do you have room?"

Sarah smiled, and held out a hand to Ruth. "We have room. Come in, and we'll show you some places where you can settle." Ruth took her hand, then hugged her. "Thank you," she whispered.

"Then we can get together," said Patrick, "get to know each other, and have a meal. From what I've been told, that was a long walk, and the day is getting hotter. Come in out of the sun."

Sarah led them into the city plaza, and pointed out the buildings around them.

"We mostly live there, in these two buildings. There's a working kitchen in the bottom of that one. These, over there and back down that street, are in good shape and no one lives there. I think twice your number could easily fit in the first two or three, and be comfortable."

"Hardy?" she called, and a lanky teenager answered.

"Would you find a couple of brooms for them? I'm guessing the rooms over there will need a bit of sweeping."

Turning back to Ruth, she pointed to the kitchen. "We'll go over there and be getting some food ready. When you've found some places you like, and put down your belongings, come on over."

Patrick stirred the stew while Sarah sliced bread and carrots. James set some bowls out on the long dining tables.

"What do you think?" asked James, "from what you've seen?"

"Don't know much about them," said Sarah, "but her apology was sincere. Not a lot more to say, I guess."

"We'll get along," said Patrick. "No bad people in that bunch, best I can tell so far. Had some hard times. And we can sure use the help, especially up in the canyons."

"You've both worked out ways of living together," said James. "Combining the groups immediately might ruffle some feathers."

"Think we should divide up the work, at least to start?"

"You're probably better with the animals," suggested James. "They look to be strong, and younger — maybe better suited to plowing, digging for minerals, that sort of thing?"

"We'll ask," said Sarah. "And do what we can to make them welcome. Are you going to stay?"

James shook his head. "Have a lot to do, so I need to be on my way soon. But I want to be sure you get a good start here."

"Thank you, sir," said Patrick, slipping a bit of Sarah's hot bread off the counter and easing down onto a bench. "I can see that might be a twisty road, and I'm a bit nervous about it."

Arthur joined them.

James motioned for Sarah to sit down as well. "Arthur, you met Jesus the day I came. Samuel has been set free from a long darkness, and he knows the King as you do. Both of you can introduce others to Him, listen to His voice leading you, and let Him be your source of knowledge and wisdom as the city grows. Just ask Him what to do, as each issue comes up. If you will all follow Him and trust him, serving each other, this will be a wonderful place to live."

Ruth and Samuel came in, and James invited them to join the group.

"We were just talking about the two groups coming together," he said. Ruth nodded.

"Samuel, you should know that Arthur has met the King, as you did."

Samuel's face shone. "It was wonderful!" he exclaimed. "I'm free!"

"There are all sorts of decisions to be made about how to divide the work and how to live together. Please lead everyone to know Him as well, and ask His guidance on everything."

"Are you leaving?" asked Samuel.

James nodded. "You will be fine, and I'll be back. Learn to walk with Him and each other! Let's go to Him now, and commit everything to Him."

James raised his hands, looked up, and said, "Father, I ask you to fill Ruth and Patrick with your love and presence, as you have done for Samuel and Arthur. Guide them, give them wisdom each day, and teach them to love You and each other."

The others at the table always said later that they felt peace at that moment, and a new hope, and their minds were drawn to a Presence in the room that was not visible to their eyes. When they finally looked around, James was gone.

New Life, New Solutions

Prove It

Amber sat in the cafe listening to the chatter around her. Most of the men, young and old, had gone to Armageddon and not returned. A few who were sick or injured had stayed, and now they, with the women, were the leadership of ... what was left.

Children were growing up, some with little memory of what was before. In some ways that was good. Memory of the horror of life under the Deceiver - no, thanks. But they would also grow susceptible to those temptations, not having the first hand knowledge of what they lead to.

So many times, we repeat our history.

"Something to eat, ma'am?"

The lady serving her looked tired. Life was different now, but hard. When the men who knew how to run the electric plant, and the factories, and repair and maintenance companies, were gone, everything changed.

"What do you have today... Lucy?" Amber made a guess at the handwritten name on the faded tag.

"Yes, ma'am, that's right!" Lucy brightened noticeably. "Thank you ma'am, that's nice, no one notices your name when you're just the waitress!"

"Lucy, no one else needs your attention right now. Please sit down for a minute." Amber motioned to the chair on the other side of the small, unsteady table. "Tell me how you are."

Lucy looked at her, frowning, as she gladly got off her feet and sighed. "How I am?"

She was silent, and Amber explained her question. "It's been a rough time, since the battle. How are you doing? You lost someone, I would guess, and have been going on without them, day by day. I'd like to pray for you, if I may."

Lucy looked at her intently, then tears began to appear in her eyes. She made no attempt to wipe them away, and they began to flow down both cheeks. Amber removed the paper napkin from her silverware and offered it. The older woman took it, held it to her eyes, and rested her elbows on the table, face buried in her hands.

Amber reached across the table and pressed her hands onto Lucy's elbows, and spoke softly. "Father, my friend needs your comfort. Bring your healing, your peace, your comfort. Open her heart to know you and receive your love."

They sat for a long moment, not moving or speaking. Minutes went by. Then Lucy took a deep, slow breath, made a final wipe of her eyes, folded the napkin neatly, and put her hands down. Looking at Amber, she smiled. "I'm better. Thank you." She glanced around, and saw people waiting for her. She stood up, and as she turned to go, said, "In fact, I'm much, much better. Grilled trout, with vegetables? It's the best we've got."

Amber smiled and nodded, and Lucy hurried off.

Amber asked for some coffee and pie when she had spent all the time she could over her meal. Finally the cafe was empty, except for Lucy and herself. Lucy came back and sat down again.

"My feet do get tired," she said sitting heavily into the chair. "Who are you? Why are you here? Where are you from?"

"I'm Amber. God sent me," Amber said simply. "A lot of healing is needed, since the war, and He sent us out to begin the process."

"Did you see it? Before the cameras all died? That invasion from outer space?"

"I was there," Amber replied. "I was part of the invasion."

Lucy stared, and shook her head. "Now don't fool with me, Amber, I'm no youngster who will believe anything you say. Tell me, very carefully, what you mean, because it makes no sense."

"You know how bad things have been, for a very long time. The evil that you have been crushed under." Lucy nodded.

"God finally dealt with it. The Deceiver is locked up, for a while. The one you saw leading the invasion is Jesus. Just like the Bible said, he came and fought for you. I was one of those in the army behind him."

"Prove it."

"How about if I just prove God sent me to you today, would that be enough?"

Lucy cocked her head and narrowed her eyes, looking as though she were trying to see into Amber's soul. "All right," she said, "do that."

"You said you are much, much better than before. Tell me about it."

Lucy's eyes looked around the ceiling, the way people do when they are thinking about something. "I'm at peace.

Haven't been peaceful inside in a long, long time. I'm not angry anymore. I'm not worried about tomorrow, and the next day, and the next. I'm ..."

She paused, closed her eyes, and did not speak for a minute or two. Then she looked straight at Amber and said, "I'm not alone."

Amber smiled. "You've met Him. You know He's here, and loves you."

Lucy nodded. "I do."

"Do you need more proof?"

Lucy leaned back in the chair, visibly relaxed, and smiled. "That's a lot, you're right. But how about one more thing?"

Amber waited.

"If God sent you, He can tell you things about me."

Amber nodded.

"So, tell me."

"Anything in particular?"

Lucy raised her eyebrows. "It's that easy?"

"Well," laughed Amber, "I only know what He tells me. But He knows what would be most significant to you, and He is glad to prove Himself to an open heart. Ask me something, and I'll ask Him."

"When was I born?"

"Something harder, please. I could guess at that, and you'd never know."

Lucy pursed her lips and nodded. "True. How about ... the name of the street where I was born?"

Amber smiled. "That's better." Amber closed her eyes. "Let's see ... your family lived on Franklin street, and the hospital they tried to get to was on Adams, but you were actually born in the car, at the corner of ... of Jackson and Summit."

She opened her eyes, and found Lucy staring with her mouth wide open. After a moment, Lucy lifted her hand to her mouth, made a big show of closing it, and sat looking at Amber. "No way you could have guessed that. I have to believe you."

"Good," said Amber. "Now, let's go a step further. You know Him too. I know by what you've said... the only way we have peace, really, is when we let His life live in us, and you've done that!"

"OK..." said Lucy, uncertainly.

"Let me show you that you can hear Him too, and you can pray for people, and we can work together to bring some healing to this city."

A door opened at the back of the cafe, and a man with the cap of a short-order cook came out. He began putting chairs up on the table.

Amber motioned at him. "Do you know where he was born?"

"No idea."

"Ask God, listen for the answer in a quiet place in your mind, and then ask ... Frankie, is that his name? ... If it's right."

Lucy frowned. "How did you know his ... OK, I got it, never mind." She laughed, then closed her eyes and said quietly, "Umm.. God? Father? Where was Frankie born?"

A startled look came over her face, and her eyes popped open. After a glance at Amber, she looked across the room and called, "Frankie?"

"Yes, Miss Lucy?" He kept putting chairs on the table.

"Were you born in Pensacola?"

Frankie stopped in the middle of lifting a chair, and set it back down. He slowly turned and walked over to them. He nodded at Amber, but focused completely on Lucy.

"There's not a person in a thousand miles knows that. I put my whole life behind me when I left there, and never said a word about it, ever since. How would you know that?"

Amber looked up at him and said softly, "Frankie, please sit down with us for a minute."

He looked back and forth between them, and then pulled a chair over and carefully sat down. He waited, obviously very nervous about the conversation.

"She wanted some proof that God is real, and that He speaks to us, and that she can hear him," explained Amber. "You came in. So I suggested that she ask God about you, and ask Him something that she absolutely did not know."

He looked at Lucy. She nodded. He looked back at Amber.

"Frankie, I would guess that there's some deep pain back there, and that when you left your life behind, it was to get away from that."

"Now wait, ma'am, whoever you are..."

Amber raised a hand. "Don't want to know anything about it, Frankie. Absolutely not. But I would like to pray for you, if you would give me your permission to do that."

"What? Pray for me? Whatever for?" He looked at Lucy, and she nodded. "Do it," she mouthed, without speaking.

He shook his head. "That's crazy."

"As crazy as God telling me something I could never have known?" asked Lucy, in almost a whisper. "Do it."

Frankie stood, and angrily tossed his chair onto a tabletop.

"No, I've had enough. Good night, ladies!" He walked to the counter, dropped his cook's apron on it, and stormed out the front door. "You can lock up," he said over his shoulder, as he threw the door closed behind him.

Amber saw the worried look on Lucy's face. "Give it time. Don't worry. We all run from our pain. Let God work with him. You and I have some things to do!"

She got up, put her chair on top of the table, and started doing the same thing at the next table over.

Lucy laughed. "You are something else! All right, let's do it." And soon the cafe was swept and the door was locked.

"Good night, Lucy."

"Good night. Will I see you again? Wait — don't answer — I owe you breakfast. Be here at eight!" insisted Lucy. And she walked away down the street.

Amber stood there for a moment, then looked up at the stars, so clearly visible in a town with no electricity to spare on streetlights.

"Thank you, Father. Always fun to watch you work!"

When Amber arrived at eight the next morning, there was a handwritten sign hanging on the doorknob by a piece of dirty string.

"Closed until lunch."

As she began to turn away, the door opened, and Lucy waved her inside without speaking. With the door closed behind them, Lucy said, "Frankie is waiting for you."

At the last table before the kitchen door, Frankie sat staring out the window. The women approached, and he looked at them.

"Please." He motioned to a chair.

"Lucy, let us talk alone?" Amber asked, and Lucy nodded, quickly disappearing out the front door.

"Sorry. I was angry."

Amber sat down, nodded, and waited.

"Can you pray for me, or do I have to tell you?"

Tears came to Amber's eyes, at the obvious pain in the man in frontof her. She shook her head, and simply reached out for his hands. He lay them down on the table, and she put hers on top of his. She began to pray in her mind and spirit, not knowing what to say out loud.

In a minute or two, Frankie began to sob. It came over him in waves, sometimes soft, sometimes full of pain and regret. After what seemed like an hour, he became silent. A few minutes later, he withdrew his hands and she opened her eyes to look at him.

Frankie was exhausted, his eyes swollen and wet, but a smile on his face. "I'm good," he said. "I'm good. Thank you."

After a moment he added, "I think I need to go home for a bit, so I can be ready for the lunch crowd. Excuse me?"

She smiled at him and nodded, holding out a hand. He squeezed her hand, and in a moment he also had disappeared through the front door. Lucy came in and hurried over to sit down with Amber.

Amber just smiled at her, shrugged, and said, "Is there any coffee yet?"

Lucy made some coffee, and sat back down. "Amber, I need to ... well, maybe I just really want to ... my husband died on that day, and my two sons. You said God dealt with the evil, and that's good, I'm glad. And you say you were there. But ... my husband ... my sons ... they weren't evil!"

"And they had no choice about being there, isn't that right?"

"That's right!" She closed her eyes, squeezing them shut.

Amber was silent, feeling that Lucy was working through the pain again, and needed a moment. When Lucy finally looked up at her, waiting for an answer, Amber reached over and took her hand.

"I'll tell you a secret. It's not over when you die."

Lucy waited, watching intently.

"The reason I was there, with Jesus, in that host behind him, is that I had already died long before that. I am part of His bride."

"When did you die? You look very alive to me!"

"Do you have Bibles? No, those were all taken, weren't they? Did anyone ever tell you about Jesus, what He did, what they did to Him?"

Lucy shook her head. "Legends, myths... bedtime stories ... probably hasn't been a Bible printed in a hundred years. I've heard about those, but I've never seen one."

"They killed Jesus, and that death, that willing sacrifice by the only innocent man the world has ever known, paid for all of us, ransomed us back from death, to belong to God. Then, three days later, He was back alive, and started showing himself to all his followers. Hundreds of them. They went everywhere, telling the world, reconciling people to God.

"Even though He's literally the son of God, He looks like a man, because He is a man. Born like the rest of us... but in a permanent, eternal body. Now I'm like that, and you will be too. And your husband, and your sons. It's not over. We were made for eternity, but this first body ..."

She poked on Lucy's arm.

"This body has to die, so the real one can come forth. Like seed in the ground, and the plant is born from it."

Lucy shook her head. "Too much. But I have something I did not have before." She smiled.

"What's that?"

"Him. I know Him. So I'm all right. I'll be OK."

"Yes," said Amber. "You'll be OK."

A Funny Accent

Amber left the cafe as the noon crowd began arriving and walked the streets of the small country town. Houses showed the need for maintenance, but the simple tasks of picking up litter, keeping things basically in order — those were all getting done.

Two kids came towards her on small bicycles. One of them seemed to be sitting almost sideways. She held up a hand, and they stopped.

"May I help you with that seat?"

The freckled face with blonde pigtails smiled back at her, and the girl hopped off. "It hurts, but I don't know what to do!"

Amber took the seat in both hands and managed to twist it back to a straight position.

"Thanks, lady! Can you come have lunch with us?"

"If your parents want me to, sure!"

"Don't go anywhere," said the older boy with her, and they pedaled back the way they had come along the street. Amber was headed that way, so she slowly walked along.

Haven't seen any cars. No gasoline, I suppose. Electricity? The stove was using gas, in the cafe... seems like there were some streetlights on last night, but not many.

But how is the dynamic in the town? Who has taken leadership, and is there any move towards knowing God?

After centuries of domination by the Deceiver, so little memory remains of things that matter.

The boy came rolling back towards her and circled around her before stopping.

"Come on!" he said. "Mommy said it was fine. It's the red house after that big rusty truck down there. And don't worry, the truck doesn't go anywhere!" He sped off, back towards the house.

When she arrived at the red house, a slender woman in an apron pushed open a screen door, stepped out and waved a hand covered in white powder. "Come on in! Working on some dough." She disappeared back into the house, and Amber walked up to the small porch, pulled open the door and slowly entered the house.

The floor was bare, the few pieces of furniture almost bare. Upholstery was worn through. No lights were on, but plenty of windows made that not a problem.

"In here," came the voice from the kitchen. At a small table the two children worked on a puzzle. "Hi!" said the girl, waving. "Mommy, that's her, she fixed my seat!"

"Thank you," said the mom, without taking her hands out of the dough. "Be through with this in a minute, then I can let it rise while we visit." White powder coated her arms up to the elbows, and splotches of it were on her face and apron.

"Sure," said Amber. "Can I help?"

"You can get us some bowls from up there," said the lady, motioning with her head to a cabinet over the sink. "Spoons are down there," and again she motioned with her head and looked at a drawer to Amber's left. "Tommy, make some room, please. Five of us!"

She pressed the dough into a pan, went to the old cast iron sink, washed her hands and arms, took off the apron, and sat down on the nearest chair. Then she stood up again, pulled a couple of glasses from the upper cabinet, and filled them with water. She put one for Amber and one for her. The kids kept working the puzzle.

"Whew. Hard on the back, after a while. But welcome. And thanks for fixin' the bike, it sure needed it. I couldn't turn it."

Then she looked more closely at Amber. "How did you turn it? That darn thing was rusted in place, and I don't see any tools in your bag! In fact ..."

She peered around Amber.
"In fact, I don't see any bag at all! Were you just out for a walk?"

"Yes, I suppose so. It turned for me, that's all I can say."

"Hmph. A miracle, that. Well, good. I'm glad, like I say, glad to have it done."

She took a long sip from the water glass. "Now ... I promised a bowl of soup! And they won't let me forget, for sure!" The boy glanced up and winked at Amber, then went back to the puzzle.

While the mom took the four bowls over to the stove top and filled them, Amber took a longer look at the puzzle. She leaned over to the girl and said, "What is it?"

"I don't know," was the answer, without looking up. "But it's pretty!" A large bird with a long pale beak looked up at

Amber, its head and back a bright red, with wings going to yellow and blue.

"Where I grew up," said Amber, "I think we called that a macaw, or some such. Like a parrot. Look at those colors!"

"Where was that?" asked the mom, bringing two bowls and setting them in front of the kids. "Where did you grow up? I don't recognize your accent at all! Tommy, move the puzzle, make room."

She set two more bowls down, steam rising from potato soup with sprinkled cheese.

"I have an accent?" said Amber. "Really?"

"Everyone has an accent, honey. You can't grow up anywhere without gettin' an accent! What's yours?"

A better question, she thought, would be 'when,' not 'where'!

"Traveled a lot," she said. "Never lived anywhere very long. How about you? Has this been home forever?"

"Pretty much. Oh, apologies, I'm Sandra. Jenkins. This is Tommy — well, you know that already, and Lindy. Your name was...""

"Amber."

"Amber what? Got a last name?"

"Not any more, I guess," laughed Amber. "Not any more. May I ask a blessing for the meal?"

"You worried about it? Think it will upset your stomach, or something?"

Amber laughed, and put a hand on Sandra's arm. "You've got so many good questions, I need to give better answers! No, just to say thank you to Father for the food."

"He can hear you? Didn't see him..."

She turned and looked to the door.

All Amber could do was smile, and shake her head. The Deceiver had wiped all knowledge of God from the face of the earth, it seemed.

"No, Sandra, I meant our Father, the God who made us, who made the whole earth and the heavens... and who is the giver of all good gifts."

Sandra looked at her for a moment. "I've never heard any such thing. You go ahead, you say thank you, and then you tell me what in this wide world you are talking about!"

As Amber said a simple table blessing, she heard steps outside, a shuffling sound, and the door pushed open. Everyone else quickly stood up and silently waited, while a heavy-set man in workman-dirty clothes made his way in.

Sandra went to him, wrapped her arms around him, and then took his sack and helped him out of a light jacket. He looked at Amber.

"I'm Amber," she said. "Just visiting."

"Where's she from," the man asked Sandra. "Funny accent!"

Amber laughed, and then Sandra laughed, and the kids laughed, and finally the man smiled sheepishly.

"Sorry. Was that rude? Just surprised me, is all."

"Want to wash up, honey? Soup's ready."

"Sure, sure," he said. "Oh, I'm Tom, if she didn't tell you that already." And he shuffled down the dark hall.

Sandra spread the chairs a bit, putting Tom's between her and the kids, and took care not to undo any of the puzzle pieces that had been assembled. She gathered up the unused puzzle pieces to make room to set the kids' bowls in front of them.

Tom was back soon and settled in. "You ain't started yet?" he said, picking up his spoon.

"Miss Amber was talking to God, before we ate. But she's done now, so we can eat now!"

"Talking to God! About what? Is he mad at us?"

"Not that I know of," smiled Amber. "Sandra, this is absolutely delicious! I know one bowl that will hardly need washing when the meal is over!"

The family was quiet for a few minutes, as everyone ate. Amber got the sense that sometimes food was a little scarce, and they appreciated it when they had it. When they offered her first choice on getting a second helping, she assured them she was fine.

"Don't eat much these days, and that was just right!"

Sandra brought the pot over and divided up the rest among them.

"So." Tom pushed his chair back, and looked at Amber.

"She fixed Lindy's bike seat," said Sandra quietly.

Tom looked at Sandra, and back at Amber. He looked at her hands.

"No tools," added Sandra.

Tom looked at Amber, and waited with raised eyebrows.

She just shrugged, then said, "You could not go to the battle?"

He shook his head. "Bad leg. Didn't want me. I'm glad, of course. And now... so many are gone ... it takes all of us to keep the simple stuff working, and no one knows how to fix the complicated stuff! I mainly work on water pipes. Got friends who figure out the electricity, best they can."

Amber nodded. "What is wrong with your leg?"

"Oh," he said, rubbing it, "hardly get any blood down there. No strength any more, and numb most of the time." He waved at his right foot and calf. "Can't hardly tell those are mine!" He smiled at Sandra, who looked up at the ceiling.

An old joke, thought Amber. How many times has Sandra heard it?

"Sandra told you I was talking with God."

He nodded.

"He sent me."

She waited a moment.

"The evil one wiped out the knowledge of God ... everywhere ... and He wants us to introduce people to Him again, now that we are free from that awful creature ... for a while."

"It's peaceful, now, it sure is," said Sandra. "Hadn't thought about that being tied somehow to the battle and all... but Tom, you know, ever since that awful day ... the darkness is gone. The hate. The ... all of it."

He nodded thoughtfully.   "Yes, ma'am, you're onto somethin'. It is indeed, and that's when it left! Sudden-like."

"So what are you doing, and who is 'us' ... that you mentioned?" Tom turned more towards her, and Amber saw the determination in his eyes to really understand what was going on.

"He loves us. Beyond what we can know, without limit. And He wants you to know that, and accept it, and begin to know Him... to really know Him as a friend, as a good father... and after we die physically, we begin a life with Him that never ends."

"I don't know what to do with that," said Tom, rubbing his face. "My family lives close to starving, I work to exhaustion every day, my body is broken down ... and there's a God who loves me?"

Amber saw an openness in him, but huge obstacles presented by the evidence of daily life.

"He came, in person, as a man, in the same part of the world where the battle took place. I don't know how to tell you when that happened... using the calendar you're using now ... "

She waved at a calendar on the wall that apparently said they were in the year 142. Counting from when?

"And he showed people his love in every way he could. Now he's sending us... people who belong to Him... to do the same thing. If you will let me, I'd like to ask him to heal your leg. Would you let me do that?"

"You want to ... to ask this God you talk to ... to fix my leg?"

"To show you, in a way you'll never forget, that what I say is true."

He began laughing, and looked at Sandra. "This is crazy! What's that story, about getting three wishes?"

Sandra was staring at Amber, a desperate hope in her eyes, a hope that was terribly afraid this was all a bad joke.

Amber watched Tom, and waited, not moving, not speaking.

"What if that's not the most important thing I need?" he finally responded, suddenly more serious.

"What is?" asked Amber.

Tom looked at Sandra, and glanced at the children. She nodded. "Tommy, Lindy, let's go for a walk. Daddy needs to talk to Miss Amber for just a minute."

They reluctantly got up and followed her out, watching Amber as they passed by. She winked at Tommy, and he flinched in surprise, then before they got out the door he winked back.

Sitting alone with Tom, Amber asked again, "What is?"

Tom clenched his jaw, and then relaxed, and almost fell back into the chair. Not looking at her, he said, "We don't have much of a doctor here, but I guess he's as smart as any that are left. He says the pain in my gut is cancer. Says I might have ... weeks? Maybe a few months? To live."

Tom swallowed hard, closed his eyes, and tears began to show. "I don't want to leave them."

He could not speak for a minute. Then he continued, "It's been hard. So hard. So many gone. And for me to leave too ... just from bein' sick ..."

He shook his head, and could say no more.

Amber knelt down in front of him, and tears began to fill her eyes as well. She placed a hand on his right knee.

"Father ... I bring my brother to you. You love him... Please give him what he asks, what he needs."

Then she prayed in the Spirit for a few minutes. She moved her hand down to the calf, speaking softly ... "here..." and then to the ankle ... "here..." and to his foot ... "and here..."

Then she put her hand on his knee, and prayed until she felt that things were finished, or at least there was no more to do, save one last thing. "Where is the pain in your stomach?"

He pointed.

She stood, and put both hands over his right abdomen, just under the ribs. Suddenly she pulled back for a moment, and said, "Oh."

She frowned, and concentrated. It seemed to be true.

"Tom, forgive me, I'm not talking to you." He nodded. She placed one hand back on his ribs, and said simply, in a loud, clear command, "Get out of here."

Tom convulsed, as though a stomach cramp had hit him.

She waited just a moment, and then spoke once more.

"Now."

He doubled over, and gagged. Just as he seemed about to throw up, it was over. Everything was quiet. He slowly straightened up, and felt of his abdomen, feeling around, pushing in various places.

He looked at her, puzzled.

"It's gone," she said simply. She held out a hand. "Let's go for a walk!"

He stared at her, then took her hand and slowly stood up. He looked down at his feet, and carefully moved his right foot, then moved it again, then stood firmly upright on both feet.

He stared at her again. She smiled, enjoying his surprise.

Then he began rocking up on his toes, and then jumping up and down. "It's gone! I can walk!"

"I'll bet you can do more than walk!" she laughed.

"I'll bet I can!" He ran out the door, shouting, "Sandra! Sandra! Look at me! Look at me! Sandra!"

Amber sat back down, tears running down her face.

She looked up. "We walk by faith, Father, we just walk by faith. Thank you for being so faithful."

What Do I Owe You?

Tom and Sandra eventually came back, holding each other tight with the two kids holding on to them as well.

As they piled through the door, a more lively bunch than they had probably been for a very long time, Tommy winked at Amber and she laughed, winking back.

"Can't thank you enough," said Tom, and tears began running down his face. "I've got to know more. Tell us everything."

Late that evening the kids were asleep on the floor, and the house grew quiet. The questions seemed to have all been asked, and Amber had prayed for them to receive their new relationship with God.

"What will you do now?" asked Sandra, trying to hold back a yawn, leaning on Tom with his arm wrapped around her. "There are so many who should know ..."

"It's really what will we do now," smiled Amber. "You know Him, too. Ask Him to suggest some next steps."

"By the way," Amber added, "Do you know the cafe downtown, where Lucy and Frankie work?"

"Of course!" said Tom. "How do you know them?"

"They met the Father yesterday. Shall we go have breakfast there tomorrow?"

At 8 am the next morning, Lindy and Tommy burst through the cafe door, ran to "Miss Lucy" and covered her up in hugs.

"We know Him, too!" they shouted. "Mommy and Daddy know Him too!"

Amber could see through the window, before she ever got into the cafe, the amazement on Lucy's face as she looked at Tom. The stooped, weary, shuffling man she had recently known walked tall and easily, with a smile that had long been missing from that familiar face.

Lucy reached out to Sandra and hugged her, and waved to an empty booth for the family to settle in. All the while her eyes did not leave Tom, until finally she realized Amber was there, and burst out laughing. "I should have known!" she exclaimed, and grabbed Amber in that same eager embrace. "I should have known," she whispered as they held each other.

A dozen others in the cafe silently watched this parade, similarly amazed. Finally an old, thin man with deep-set eyes and thick white hair stood up from a table at the window and walked slowly over to Tom. As he reached the booth, Tom sprang up and shook his hand eagerly.

"Doc, I'm well! I can walk! Look!" Tom danced a little jig in a circle. "And the pain is gone, completely gone!" He slapped his stomach. "I'm well!"

Doc looked around at the family, and glanced at Amber. "That's wonderful, Tom," he said in a slow, amazed voice, staring at him. "How did it happen? Is it real?"

"You'll have to ask her," smiled Tom, and waved him over to Amber. But Amber just shrugged, and said, "You can tell him."

Doc looked back at Tom, and every face in the cafe did the same. Everyone waited.

Tom looked at Amber, and nodded. He took a deep breath and turned to face Doc.

"There's a God in Heaven," he began slowly. And for the next ten minutes, he told Doc and everyone else in the cafe about the King.

"And?" said Doc, eyebrows raised. "What does all that have to do with you, and the cancer being gone, and your leg being healed?"

"Cancer," whispered a voice across the room, and two or three more said the word again. Tom looked around, and said it out loud, for the first time. "I had cancer."

"Right, Doc?" He spoke loudly, and made it a public conversation.

"That's right. And it is past the point where anything can be done about it."

"Then Amber came." He looked at her, then looked around the room. "She told us about the King, just as I've now told all of you. And then she asked him, asked God, to heal me."

He raised his arms, and danced the little jig again, with his arms high above is head. "And he did!"

Tommy and Lindy clapped, and everyone laughed.

"Nonsense!" said Doc, his face tight and red. "That ... is ... nonsense. It will be back!" And he stormed out of the cafe.

In the silence that followed, Tom stared after him, then turned to Amber.

"Will it be back?" he whispered, worry on his face.

"No," she said quietly. "It looked like cancer, it pretended to be cancer, but it was not cancer. And it is gone. Forever."

Turning to face the others in the cafe, she said, "Everything Tom told you is true. I'll be glad to tell you more, and answer any questions. There's no hurry. But now, let's get some breakfast for this family!"

She waved to Lucy and squeezed into the booth next to Tommy. With a wink.

When the family had eaten and gone, and Tom had left for work, Amber sat stirring a coffee, feeling that there was more to come.

A slender, middle-aged man came to her, and waved to the opposite seat in the booth. "May I?"

She nodded, and waited. Lucy came with the coffee pot, looked at Amber's cup, and laughed. "You're not half through that cup, and you've been here all morning!"

Amber looked at it, and up at Lucy. "It's so good, I hate to hurry!"

Lucy shook her head. "Steve, I'll bring you a fresh cup. You're done with your plate?"

Steve nodded, and Lucy went to gather his dishes from the table across the cafe.

Amber waited, wondering where this new conversation would take them.

"I have a book," he said, watching her expression. "A very old book. Some of the pages are still readable, and even on those pages, I don't know what some of the words mean. But it talks about a man named Jesus. And I think it tells some of what he said and did. Is that who you're talking about?"

She nodded, now smiling. A rare book indeed, these days.

"And you know him?"

She nodded again. "And so can you."

"But that was ... Centuries ago? And they killed him."

"And three days later ..."

He waited, and she could tell he did not know the end of the story.

"Three days later He walked out of that cave, that tomb, alive again forever, and after talking to hundreds of people over several weeks, He returned to Heaven. Centuries later, he led the armies of Heaven to defeat the 'Leaders' in the great battle."

"That was the same man?" He stared at her. "How can you know him now? How can anyone?"

Amber turned and caught Lucy's eye. "Can you join us?"

"Let me guess," said Lucy as she slipped into the booth. "You're talking about my new Friend."

Amber smiled. "Steve ... Is that right? ... Steve would like to know how anyone today can know Him."

"I met Him yesterday, sitting right over there," she pointed. Then she told him what had happened.

"And to prove I really knew Him, she gave me a test. And He told me something I could never have guessed! I really did hear His voice.... And I guess the point is, so can you."

She looked at Amber. "Did I do good?"

The both laughed. "You did good! Thank you," said Amber.

Lucy squeezed Steve's arm and excused herself.

"Well ... I'm sure going to think about it. How long will you be around?"

"Not sure. If you can read much in that wonderful book, you'll see that He basically followed the Father's prompting, day by day, doing whatever He saw the Father leading Him to do, and that's what we do now. It's pretty unpredictable."

"And what is that, for you... or for 'us', whoever that is?"

"Putting things back together, and leading people to know Him. The evil that was so recently removed will return, sooner than we'd like, and we want to restore the knowledge of God to the world before that happens."

"A big job."

She waited.

"Let me ask you about something else, then," he continued. "Does 'putting things back together' include restoring the normal things needed for people to live and work together? Basic stuff like water and electricity, and more complicated things like laws, financial arrangements, schools, hospitals, all that?"

She nodded, and waited.

"How can you do that?"

"Through people like you, I think. People who see the need and are willing to ask God for His answers, instead of creating more mess. What part of that do you feel most urgent about?"

He traced a design on the tabletop. "Perhaps money," he said, looking up. "Everyone can do something, and money enables them to be paid for that thing, and be able to buy what they need from others... So it gives a way to balance the value of a two eggs and a cup of coffee against the value of 4 hours of carpenter work. You understand."

"How is Lucy being paid, here?"

"We do things for each other, and don't worry so much about the balance. Tom helps with plumbing, others help with electrical things, I do a little work with wood, making and fixing things ... So we each do what we can, and ask for what we need from whoever might be able to provide it."

"Is it working?"

"Mostly. But that breaks down pretty quickly, because of distance, lack of relationship, lack of trust or reliable commitments... All sorts of reasons. Some people need things and don't contribute anything back. I think pretty soon a neutral 'token of value' will be needed, something that everyone can earn and spend."

"You've been thinking about this. Are you a teacher?"

"Used to be. So I have books, and have read about ancient life, before the ... you know. Before the tyrants."

"I do know. I remember, in fact."

He looked up at her sharply. "You... remember? I'm at least 20 years older than you, maybe 30, and that was long, long before my time!"

"Thanks for the compliment. I'll explain later. But what would you suggest, for this 'token of value'? I think God may have already been talking to you about it."

He shook his head. "Don't know about that, but ... It's really pretty simple. Just has to be something that's limited in quantity, something you can't easily make more of ... So the value of each piece of it stays roughly constant, and no one can just go home and make more of it."

"And one piece of it has to be worth a small amount, so it could be used to pay for ... a cup of coffee," he continued, looking into her cup. "Even one that lasts all day!"

She looked for Lucy and held it up in the air. "It's good. I'll get some more, and maybe we'll figure out how to pay for it!"

"I think you've paid your bill for a long time to come," he laughed. "When she brings you more, you can ask her."

Lucy brought the pot and filled Amber's now empty cup.

"What do I owe you?" asked Amber.

Lucy frowned at her, looked at Steve, and just shook her head as she left.

"See? That's how it works here!"

"I like it," smiled Amber. "I really do. But you're right, of course. Got anything in mind?"

"Seems like all sorts of things have been used in the past, in ancient history, and it changed from time to time. Whatever each culture could make work, for at least a while..."

"I believe God is giving you some wisdom about this, and it will be a need everywhere. Maybe local solutions at first, and eventually something more widespread. We'll talk again, I'm sure. In the meantime, is there anything I can pray for you about?"

He pursed his lips, and leaned back.

"I guess the place to start is just ... for me to know Him. Would you agree?"

Putting Things Back Together

It's Called Work

Jeff stood on a downtown corner of what used to be a sprawling, bustling city. Nothing moved but the crumpled paper blown along the street by a cold wind, but he could easily imagine the buses rushing by, the crowds of people filling the intersection when the lights were red, the quick stops and quick starts of all the lanes of cars when they turned green again.

But now ... nothing.

His arms were grabbed from behind and his elbows squeezed together behind him.

Andar stood across the intersection, nine feet tall and glowing, waiting to see if Jeff wanted help. He shook his head. Whoever was behind him could not see Andar, obviously, and Jeff would have been very surprised if they could.

"Hi," he said quietly. "Something I can do for you?"

"Whatever money you got, I'll take it."

"If I had any," said Jeff. "What else?"

"Got a knife? A ring? Anything I can sell?"

"No, don't think so. These sandals are pretty worn, and what you see on me is all I've got on. So, what else can I do for you?"

The man pushed him away, and Jeff turned around. Two boys stood there, in their late teens at most.

"What are you doing robbing people? The ones who used to make you do that are gone."

The boys looked at each other. "It don't seem the same, for sure," said the shorter one, standing further away. "Why we doing this, Joey?"

"Shut up," said Joey. "It's what we do. But now, we can keep stuff ourselves, instead of giving it to Fatso."

"Joey, I'm Jeff. And you are?" He looked at the other boy.

After hesitating, the boy answered, "Bo."

"Hi. Listen, no one's here anymore, there's no one to rob. Why are you here?"

"Why are you here, yourself? Never seen you before."

"Just got here. Is Fatso still around, still making you do stuff?"

"No. They took him, when everyone left. We're ... just us."

"Any place open, any stores or anything? Can I buy you something to eat?"

"Yeah, mister, that would be great!" said Bo. "Down that way, and it smells really good in there!"

Jeff laughed. "Well, let's go, then!"

Joey did not move. "You said you got no money."

"I don't."

"How are you gonna buy us anything?"

"I don't know. But my Father said not to worry about that kind of thing, that He will take care of us. Come on!"

Joey fell in alongside, and Jeff tried to keep up with Bo. "But I don't see no one here with you. Your father? Is he here?"

"He's always here, Joey. He made the world, and He loves us. Loves you."

"Don't give me none of that stuff!" scoffed Joey. "Been on the street my whole life. Ain't no one loves me, for sure!"

"What about William?"

Joey stopped in mid-step. Jeff walked a little further, and said, "You coming?"

Joey followed, but at a distance. When Jeff got to the bakery Bo had disappeared into, he waited at the door. Joey slowly came through the door, but very carefully stepped around Jeff and watched him closely.

Bo was at the counter, staring at iced pastries and cookies.

"Bo, let me ask you something. When was the last time you had a good meal?"

"Never!" he said instantly. "But I had some oatmeal day before yesterday. Nothing since then."

"Do you have sandwiches, soup, something we can give this boy before we get to dessert?" Jeff asked the frowning man watching them from across the counter.

"Yeah, we could do that," he said. "But these boys have stolen from me lots of times. Why should I feed them?"

"That's a good question, my friend."

He turned to Bo and Joey. "What's the answer?"

Bo looked at Joey, his eyes pleading. "Joey, I'm hungry!"

Joey's angry eyes looked back and forth between the store owner and Jeff. Finally he pointed at Jeff, and said, "He's paying."

"Oh," said the owner.

"Name's Jeff, what's yours?"

"Johnson."

"Mr. Johnson, is there something I can do for you, to pay for some food for these... gentlemen?"

"You don't got any money, either?"

"How about that kitchen? Anything need doing back there?"

"Yeah, it's an awful mess. I'm waiting until you guys quit wasting my time, so I can go clean it up."

"If we clean it up for you, would that be enough to give these guys a sandwich and a cookie, and maybe something to drink?"

"It's a mess, I told you. And they never worked ten minutes in a day."

"How about it?"

Johnson looked at him. "If even one plate or glass is broken, the deal is off?"

"Sound fine," said Jeff. "Come on, guys!" And he walked into the kitchen.

It was, indeed, a mess. But Jeff's father had been a short-order cook, and he knew what to do with a commercial kitchen. He got some hot, soapy water going into the sink, and as Joey and Bo slowly wandered into the kitchen, he put them to work.

Thirty minutes later they came back out, and the boys sat down at a table, flopping down as if they had worked a ten-hour shift.

"Take a look, sir. I think you'll be happy." Jeff smiled at him and waited. Johnson went quickly through the door, and just as quickly came back out.

"You're hired," he said. "And I'm sure about who did all the work!"

"No, actually, you'd be wrong about that. In fact ... I'm not looking for work, but they are!"

Joey and Bo started protesting, but Jeff held up a hand. "Would you like to have something to eat, three times a day, and some money to buy things without stealing it, and a clean, dry place to sleep?"

"Yeah," said Bo, staring. "How would that happen?"

Jeff laughed. "It's called work. You do things for people, and they pay you. And if you work for a place that makes food, you probably don't have to spend the money you earn on food... you can spend it on other things. Like shoes, for example," he finished, pointing to Bo's bare feet.

"Let me get you what I promised, before I fall down laughing," said Johnson. "What would you 'gentlemen' like?"

Wave Your Hands

As they left, Johnson called after them, "Be here by the time the first customer finishes eating in the morning, remember!"

Joey stared at the sky. "What have I done?"

"You'll like it," said Bo. "He cooks good, and I really do want some shoes!"

"Not many people live around here," said Jeff, looking at the tall, empty buildings around them. "Surprised he has enough customers. Where does everyone live?"

"Come on, I'll show you, said Joey, looking behind them. "The bus is coming."

The walked over to the sidewalk. An ancient city bus slowly rolled up to them, coasting to a stop in the middle of the street as though the driver were trying to use as little gas as he could, and not to use the brakes at all.

"Hey, Joey," called the driver. "Gonna rob some people in the park?"

"Yeah," said Joey, slapping palms with the driver as they got in. "Thought I'd start with you! Phil, Jeff. Jeff, Phil."

Jeff shook his hand as they climbed on. "We owe you anything?"

"Only if you can pay. And he can't so ... can you?"

"He got no money," shouted Joey, "But he can do things. He'll wash your tires for you!"

"What can I do for you, Phil? Be glad to pay, but he's right. Don't have any money."

"Can you wave your hands and fill my gas tank?"

"Never tried it before. But God sent me to show people he loves them, and sometimes that means giving them what they need. Sounds like you need gas."

"Diesel, man, lots of it. They bring it in from someplace far away, I guess, and it's all I can do to have enough paying customers to afford the next tank!"

"Doesn't leave much for food and such, I guess!"

"There's a reason I'm still wearing this shirt a week later, apologies to the ladies!"

The bus rumbled out of the downtown canyons, past three-story and four-story office buildings and apartments, and finally reached what used to be a fountain in the middle of a circular road. Four roads came into the circle, and they took the third one around. It led to a park with hundred-year-old, enormous trees, and more weeds than grass. People walked here and there, some sat on blankets, and it seemed everyone there had at least one dog with them.

In the middle of the park a hill rose up, and beyond it was an outdoor stage. Off to the side was a garden, perhaps a rose garden, so overgrown it was hard to tell. But there were roses by the hundreds, maybe thousands, so Jeff guessed that must be the history of this particular garden.

Phil parked the bus and helped the few passengers get off, then shuffled to a park bench and sat heavily. Jeff sat next to him. Joey and Bo headed off in something of a hurry, but said nothing.

"Phil, that's west, right?" Jeff pointed behind them.

Phil nodded.

"You know this bench pretty well, I'm guessing."

"Why do you think so?"

"Because if that's west, then the shade of this tree will cover us in about 10 minutes, and keep it cool here for all afternoon."

Phil leaned back, closed his eyes, and nodded. "You're a smart young man. Except for hanging out with Joey. So what is this about God, and love, and all that nonsense? And are you going to wave your hands over my gas tank?" He peered at Jeff out of mostly closed eyes, then closed them and leaned back again.

"The past many years have been hell on earth, haven't they?"

"Amen."

"Have you noticed the evil, the tyranny, the constant pressure to live in the dark ... is gone?"

Phil turned and looked at him. "And?"

"Do you think that's an accident?"

"No," said Phil, finally. "It happened when the battle happened. The cameras died, so we couldn't see what happened, but ... that's when everything changed."

"God did that," said Jeff. "For you. For everyone. To give the people left on earth a thousand years, starting now, to make a better decision than to follow that beast. And to heal the land, heal the world."

"What happens in a thousand years? Not that any of us will be around..."

"The Deceiver gets out, and makes one more run at destroying all God's people."

Phil rubbed his face. "So ... assuming any of that is true ... what does it have to do with you?"

"He sent me... and others, of course ... to explain what was happening, and to offer everyone the chance to know Him. To know our real Father."

"You know Him?"

"I do."

"And I can know him, and talk with him, like you and me sitting here talking?"

Jeff nodded. "He offers an exchange. It's a contract, a covenant, actually a blood covenant, the most serious kind ... between a king and a beggar." He peered at Phil. "He's the king, we're the beggars."

"Yeah, I got that part," laughed Phil. "So what's the deal?"

"His life for yours. You get to live forever, loved by the God who made you, who made the stars. And He gets ... you, and the mess you've made of your life."

"Straight up, one for one, even trade?"

"Straight up, forever. He belongs to you, you belong to Him. Welcome to the castle."

"Prove it."

"How?"

"That tank is so empty I don't think it will even start again. Fill it up. Wave your hands."

Jeff leaned back on the bench and laughed. "So this is how He felt!"

Phil waited, an eyebrow raised.

"Jesus is God's son, and He's the one who paid for your life with His own blood. When He was beginning to gather some followers in Israel, two of them went to get a fellow named Nathaniel to join them. When Nathaniel came, Jesus said to him, 'Before Philip called you, I saw that you were under the fig tree.' Nathaniel said, 'Teacher, you are the Son of God!' So Jesus said, 'You have faith because I told you I saw you under the fig tree? You shall see greater things than these!'"

Jeff laughed again. "So here we are, thousands of years later, and people are still the same. You would have faith because of a tank of diesel fuel? 'You will see greater things than these!'"

Phil smiled. "Yeah, OK, that's pretty small, I guess. But it is what I need, and you said ... 'giving them what they need.'"

Jeff put his hand on Phil's arm, looked up, and said, "Father, thank you. Thank you for laughter, thank you for friends. Thank You for loving us. Thank you for Phil, for bringing him through some awful times. And thank you for diesel gas in the bus!"

"Jeff. It's Jeff, right?"

Jeff nodded.

"You didn't wave your hands."

"The problem with waving my hands, Phil, is that if I wave my hands, that will become 'the way you do it'. And you and everyone else will always say, 'It won't work unless you wave your hands,' and of course people will argue over which hand it was."

Phil pursed his lips and nodded. "Yeah, I see that."

"And it's God who does things, anyway, not me!"

"So... is He going to do it?"

"He loves you. Did we ask Him?"

"Uh, no, actually I noticed you did not. You just said 'thank you'."

Jeff smiled. "Go start your bus."

Phil stood up, keeping his eyes on Jeff, then slowly turned and walked ten paces to the bus door. He stood there, and finally said, "We have a deal, don't we? If I have gas, then ... this Jesus has a new follower. Is that what just happened?"

"I like it, Phil, I like it! Yes. I believe that was the deal."

Phil shook his head slowly, and climbed into the bus. After a few moments there was the sound of an old starter motor kicking cylinders into action, and the bus roared to life.

Phil sat in the bus for at least ten minutes, staring at the dashboard, as the engine purred like an old, sleepy cat on grandma's lap. Finally he turned it off, climbed out, and came back to the bench.

"How much is there, in the tank?"

"You know... Jeff... that's a funny thing. That gauge has not worked in twenty years. I just tap on the tank, and I can tell when it's about empty."

He looked at Jeff.

"The gauge says full."

He leaned over, put an arm around Jeff's shoulders, and hugged him. Then he pulled his arm back, and sat looking straight ahead.

"Guess you better tell me about this Jesus fellow, now that ... now that I belong to him."

Got Any Money?

The next day, Phil came by to pick up the boys on the way to the park.

"I want to introduce you to someone, Jeff."

Jeff climbed on. "Sure."

"Where are the guys?"

"They have a job now. Didn't tell you?"

Phil stared at him, not putting the bus into gear.

"They? Joey, and Bo? Have a job?"

"Can't believe they didn't tell you. Working at the bakery. Want to get something to eat?"

Phil looked back at the three ladies at the rear of the bus, and the older gentleman staring out the window. "What do you think? Breakfast stop?"

"No money, man," said the older fellow, without looking.

"Sure!" said a lady in a brightly flowered dress. "Haven't been there in weeks!"

"Come on, my friend," called Jeff to the gentleman. "I'll cover for you."

He turned slowly to look at Jeff. "No one does that."

"First time today."

When the bus eased to a stop, Jeff walked back to the row where the older fellow was seated and held out a hand. "Name's Jeff. Yours?"

"Kenneth, young man. Kenneth Robinson."

He picked up his hat from the seat next to him and slowly stood, moving to the aisle. "Sorry. Bones don't unbend like they used to. I was a runner, young man. You can't tell it now, by looking, so I have to tell you myself or you won't know."

"Ran the 440, I'll bet, and some relays. Went to State?"

Kenneth stopped and looked closely at him. "You just guessing? 'Cause you're guessing mighty good."

"Congratulations, Kenneth. Used to run a bit myself, but never got that far."

The ladies were all lined up in the aisle. "Are we going to eat, or just talk?"

Jeff held Kenneth's elbow and helped him down the bus steps. Then he offered a hand to the lady in the flowered dress. "Help you down?"

"Well, aren't you the gentleman! "What's your name, young fella?"

"He said, 'Jeff', Rosie!" said the woman behind her. "Pay attention, instead of talking all the time!"

"Don't help her down," said Rosie. "She doesn't deserve it."

"None of us deserve it, really," smiled Jeff, as he offered a hand to the next lady. "And you are?"

"'Sally May'," if you must know. But 'Sally' will do fine."

The third lady had not spoken, so as he reached a hand up to help her, Jeff asked, "Your name, ma'am? I'm Jeff, as you know."

"Linda, sir." She was carefully studying the steps and taking them one at a time, so he decided this was not the time be in deep conversation. "Thank you," she said quietly, as she reached the curb and let go of his hand. The others were walking to the bakery, and she turned to follow.

Phil stayed back, and walked alongside Jeff to bring up the end of the parade. "How you gonna pay for Kenneth's food? You still don't have any money, as far as I know."

"Well... " Phil looked up to the top of the bus, where Andar was stretched out. "You wouldn't have any money, would you?"

Phil looked at him, then up at the roof of the bus, then back to him. "Someone up there? Do I need glasses?"

"Actually, you can probably tell he's there. An angel. You can feel him more than see him, I would guess. If you close your eyes and just try to sense if there's someone close by ... someone big ... "

Phil closed his eyes, and almost jumped. "Good grief." He opened his eyes and stared up. "He's there, I can tell. But ... invisible?"

"To most people."

Jeff reached a hand up to mid-air, closed it, and brought it back down. "Thanks, Andar."

Jeff began walking to the bakery, and Phil hurried to catch up, looking over his shoulder. "Did he give you something?"

Jeff opened his hand. A diamond sparkled in the sun.

"You could buy the bakery with that!"

They reached the bakery, opened the door, and smelled the pastries and bread as they walked in. The ladies were all seated at a corner table with Rosie talking away. The boys were behind the counter listening to Johnson explain what was in the displays. Kenneth was walking slowly up and down the counter, inspecting each item, as though he were making the most important decision of his life and would only have one chance to make it.

"Johnson?" Jeff motioned to the owner to come over for a private conversation.

"The boys working out OK?"

"Yeah, they're actually pretty smart. Only have to say things once, and they get it. If they'll stick around, and I have enough customers to pay them, it could be a good deal for all of us."

"Here," said Jeff, holding out his hand.

Johnson took what was offered, and stared at it. He looked up at Jeff. "Is this real?"

Jeff nodded. "I'd like to make an investment in your store. More people will come, and you'll need to get more supplies, more equipment, maybe some more space. Hire some more people. This will get you started."

"You want to be, like, a partner? Is that it?"

"No, just want you to have enough money to do what needs to be done. Don't tell anyone. Oh, and one other thing... maybe that could pay for the meal, every time someone says, 'Jesus sent me.' Starting with Kenneth, there, because I told him I would pay his bill today."

Johnson shook his head. "Of course, of course. And you'll have to tell me who this Jesus is."

"Young man?" said Kenneth, waving to Johnson. "May I have one of those, if this fellow can afford it... like he said he would?"

Jeff walked over to him. "Kenneth, you may have two of them, if you like, and coffee to go with it. And anytime you come in here and say, 'Jesus sent me', your bill is paid."

Kenneth looked back and forth between Jeff and Johnson, who simply smiled and nodded.

"Thank you," he said, and slowly moved to a chair.

"Bo!"

"Yes, sir?" said the young boy, hustling out of the kitchen. "Two of the bear claws for the gentleman with the hat, and fresh coffee!"

"Yes, sir! ... Umm ... which one is the bear claw, again? The one over here, that looks like a ... oh, I got it, never mind!"

Jeff stepped up close to Johnson. "If you need more, to pay for the people Jesus sends, just let me know. I think you'll be able to find me."

"One thing, though... if you don't mind?" Johnson lowered his voice. "What makes you think more people will come?"

"Things will change. Jesus sent me to help the city, and when He walks in ... things change."

"Will he walk in? How will I know him?"

"I think you'll know those who belong to Him, and wherever they are, He's there too. That's a promise He made a long time ago, and it is more true now than ever."

"How do you ... 'belong to him'?"

"Phil can explain it to you." Jeff waved Phil over. "Maybe when he drops everyone off this afternoon, he'd have some time to talk. What do you think?" he said, turning to Phil.

Phil nodded. "I got it. First thing is, I'm gonna tell you where that money came from, and you'll never believe it!"

Jeff laughed. "'Never' is a long time, Phil! No telling what he'll believe by the time forever comes!"

What Do You Need?

As the bus pulled away and headed for the park, Jeff was sitting in the front seat close to Phil.

"You said you wanted me to meet someone? Who?"

"Oh, yeah, thanks.   He kind of runs the place. The city. Took the lead, when all the chaos happened, and suddenly no one knew what to do. Franklin. You'll like him."

After the bus was empty and the ladies had gotten seated on the shady bench, Phil and Jeff got back in the bus.

"Just a little further. See those trees across the road, and the brick buildings?"

Jeff looked. A handsome campus, it appeared.

"Used to be a university, I hear. Most of the buildings are empty, but the one closest to us is used for some offices. He's generally there. Comes to the park to meet people, see what's happening, offer some guidance, whatever... but this time of day, I think he'll be there."

"Elected, somehow, or just helping as he can?"

"Mostly that.   We talk about having elections now and then, but everyone's pretty content with how it is now... and think that when you start electing people, you get problems."

Jeff nodded. He could certainly understand that.

"But when some people start pushing on others ... what happens?"

"That's sort of where we are. That all stopped, after ... the battle ... when we were just trying to figure out how to survive. But now I think we'll have to do something."

"Speaking of that... how did you, and Johnson for that matter, stay here? Why were you not dragged off to Armageddon?"

"I was so sick I couldn't walk, could hardly speak. Some disease, everyone was getting it. Took my wife, almost took me. But by the time I could crawl out of bed, they had all gone, and I watched it from here... like everyone else."

"And Johnson?"

"Had broken his leg, I think, something. Didn't know him much then, but something like that."

The bus pulled up in the empty parking lot next to the brick two-story building. "That door," said Phil, and they got out.

The grass was well-trimmed, Jeff noticed, and flowerbeds had been planted. Why were things tended here, but not across the street in the park?

They opened the double glass doors and stepped into air conditioning.

"Nice," said Jeff. "Do all the buildings have this?"

"Just a few," said Phil. "Not many still know how to make it work, fix leaks, and all that... and not much electricity to go around, so ... some have lights and air, most don't. It does get hot here, though. It does."

They walked down a quiet, carpeted hallway, and came to an open door. Inside was a small office, a desk and some cabinets, and fresh flowers on a table with some chairs.

The next door opened into a large room with a work desk at one end and a table that could seat 20 or more filling most of the room. A man sat at the small desk, reading a huge book that looked ancient.

"Mr. Franklin, sir?"

He looked up, and carefully marked his place before setting the book down. He quickly came around the side of the desk and waved at the big oaken table. "Please, sit down, sit down."

They took seats in the soft, rolling chairs at one end of the table.

"This is where we gather people to talk about things," he said, "when things need talking about. You are?"

"Jeff, sir. God sent me to help."

Phil smiled, and Franklin showed no reaction at all.

"What sort of help?"

"What do you need?"

Franklin sat back and laughed. "That's the best offer I've had in a long time!"

He looked at Phil. "Where did you find such a jewel?"

"He found me, actually."

Franklin looked carefully at Jeff. "You know what the world has been through, lately ... I'm sure."

Jeff nodded.

"We are trying to put things back together, but there are so many missing pieces. So far, everyone is getting along all right. We have a few doctors, a few engineers, all of that. But it won't last long. We've got to start training people to do all that ... and it would be nice to figure out what to do about money."

"There hasn't been any ... right?" asked Jeff.

"Yeah, they controlled all that. You had whatever showed up in your account, you spent your day doing whatever they said, and ... you paid whatever they said the price was, for whatever they said you could buy."

He shook his head. "I think the relief of being out from under that has carried us this far. But it can't last."

"What was your role, Franklin?"

"I made shoes. Had no skill. An awful shoemaker. But that's what they made me do."

"What happened if you did not do... what they said?"

"People started disappearing. Your wife, your kids ... it was like they punished everyone around you, instead of you. It was worse that way, and obviously ... they knew it."

"Thank you, Father," said Jeff quietly.

"Father?" Asked Franklin. "Your father ... had something to do with that?"

"Your father and mine, the God who made the world and everything in it. He's the one who finally dealt with it, and brought us a time of peace, and time to ... to do exactly what you're doing. Put it back together, but in a good way, a healthy way... and to spread the knowledge of Him in the earth."

"Well, if anyone ever knew anything about him, it's gone now! I have no idea who you're talking about."

"I'll tell you all I can, but first ... I need to figure out how I can help. What are you studying?" Jeff waved at the desk with the big book spread out on it.

"Electrical engineering. We need to get power flowing to the city, so people can have lights, and cook, and ... and study!"

"You have a few people doing that now? Making electricity?"

"We have a dam close by, and the power keeps flowing through the wires from it. I guess it will, as long as the river flows. But these things keep failing, these ... transformers? ... And sooner or later, whatever is further back, between us and the dam, will start failing. I'm trying to figure out how that all works, and how to fix it. So, for now, we have a few people who know how to fix the wires, and even replace a transformer ... but that just moves the problem."

"And that's dangerous, if you don't know how it works."

Franklin nodded. "We found that out."

"What's your role?" Jeff asked.

Franklin looked at Phil, who just shrugged.

"Peacemaker? Counselor? Predictor of problems?"

Jeff nodded. He liked this man a lot, of course, and saw what an enormous influence he was having on the people around him.

You Can Do More

"To start," said Jeff, pushing his chair back, "I think I would like to pray for you. I want to ask Father to give you an abundance of insight ... the ability to understand things ... and wisdom ... the ability to know what to do about them!"

"You do that!" said Franklin. "I don't know who you're going ask for that, but I am a ready customer!"

Jeff stood behind Franklin's chair, put his hands on the man's shoulders, and began to speak quietly. After a few minutes he returned to his seat.

"Should I feel different?" asked Franklin.

"I have no idea," laughed Jeff. "God gives what He gives, and the experience of getting to know Him is different for everyone. But I think things will be different."

"You keep saying that," said Phil. "And it keeps being true!"

Franklin looked hard at Phil. "My friend, I think you need to take that book I've been reading, and then come back and tell us what we need to do. I can get someone else to drive that bus. You can do more for us ... and suddenly I am very sure what that is!"

He got up quickly, went to the outer desk, and opened and closed several drawers. "Here it is!" he called, and returned with a name badge with a safety pin on the back of it.

Phil looked at it. "Manager, Engineering Department?"

Franklin beamed. "What do you think? In fact, go look in the closets back behind that secretary's desk, and find a shirt that looks sort of official, like someone who works for the city. I think there's a lot of that sort of thing."

"Yeah, this shirt needs changing, no doubt about that!" Phil laughed, and got up to go explore the closets.

Franklin sat back down.

"Maybe this 'God' you mentioned has done something," he said quietly to Jeff. "I don't remember ever being so sure about a decision, or making one so quickly... but I think that is exactly the right thing to do!"

"Good," said Jeff. "Now let's talk about money. What are people doing now, about buying and selling things?"

"Mostly it's just good faith, and people helping people. There is some money lying around. Have you seen any of it?"

Jeff shook his head.

"But mainly it's large amounts, nothing you would spend to just buy coffee, or a pair of shoes. There's nothing we can give people that can be used to just take care of normal stuff."

"But those still work."

"Yes, but for how long? It's hard to get paid with that, and then go do anything with it, except another very large purchase."

"Can you create something?"

"We could ... but for anything we use ... rocks, paper money, pieces of anything ... it needs to be controlled. If anyone can make it, that won't work. It won't be worth anything."

"But now," said Jeff, "they just agree that a sheep is worth two pair of shoes, and a shirt is worth so many pounds of beef?"

"That's it," said Franklin, "barter and generosity."

"Have you talked to other cities around, about doing something everyone could share?"

"I have. Went to several of them. But it's hard to find the right people to talk to ... no one elects anyone to any position, from fear of control ... and no one is willing to make such a decision. And, of course, what would it be? Haven't heard any good ideas yet."

"Do you have any printing presses that are usable?"

"Hmm. I'm sure there are some... in some of these old buildings, there must have been printing companies."

"Perhaps a design could be created that would be difficult to copy, and an agreement to make only so much, so a value is maintained."

"Maybe so."

Franklin was quiet for a minute. Phil came back in a blue short-sleeve shirt that fit him perfectly, and the name tag was pinned above the pocket.

'You look great, Mr. .... Phil, How long have I known you? I don't even know your last name!"

"Mr. Phil will be just fine, Mr. Franklin!" He beamed.

"Now - can you find a replacement for driving the bus?"

"Sure. But it will take me a while to read that book!"

"Find your replacement first," said Franklin. "Then come work here, where you can concentrate. And we can figure out what to do, as you get the hard stuff worked out."

"Have you been to the dam, to see what condition things are in?" asked Jeff.

The lights in the office went dark, and the faint sound of the air conditioning fans stopped.

"I think we're about to," laughed Franklin. "Want to come?"

Getting to the Dam

"What about water?" asked Jeff, as the bus rumbled out of the city and into the foothills of the surrounding mountains.

"Same story," replied Franklin from across the aisle. "Phil, you know where we're going?"

"Never been there, boss, but I understand you take the Sharpsville road and keep turning right."

"There you go," said Franklin. More than I knew."

Jeff leaned out the window and looked up. "Having fun up there?" He laughed at the response. "We'll find something for you to do! Don't want you bored!"

"All right, I give up," said Franklin. "Who's up there?"

"Ever met an angel?"

Franklin shook his head. "God, angels ... how big does this story get?"

Jeff smiled. "Very, very big, and it goes on forever."

Phil took a right turn onto a much steeper road, then stopped. "Boss?"

Everyone looked out the windshield, where an enormous pine lay across the road, and under the pine lay a span of heavy electrical wires.

"Maybe we've found today's problem," said Phil.

They climbed out of the bus.

"Could be dangerous on that side, guys. And look over here..."

On the downhill side of the fallen tree, they could see loose wires.

"If there's power in those lines..." Franklin pointed to the ones running under the tree. "Then the bare ends could kill us. Looks like they got pulled loose from... up there."

A tall, stripped tree trunk rose above them about a hundred yards away, and big cylinders hung on each side of the tree.

"I'm thinking these wires need to get fastened back to that pole, however it works," said Phil. "Who knows how to do that?"

"Two guys you can find in town, Randy something and Fred Silverman. They know how to fasten the wires, anyway, but ...we need to kill the power coming to them, and before that, get this tree off them!"

"And they might have been pulled loose up there, as well," said Jeff, pointing to the next connection uphill. "That tree looks like it got pulled a little this way."

"Franklin, I can't believe such a big city was getting electricity from these wires. There must be something else."

He looked up and down hill, and nodded. "Maybe this isn't today's problem, but just one of many. We should keep going."

Andar? Can you help us with this tree? The answer was immediately there in his mind.

"Gentlemen, please come back into the bus." Phil and Franklin looked at him. Phil smiled, and immediately went to the bus door. "Come on, Franklin, don't wait around when he's got an idea." Franklin followed, looking very puzzled.

"I've asked my friend from on top of the bus to help us with the tree," Jeff explained. They settled into their seats and looked out the windshield. The tree was gone.

"What?" exclaimed Franklin. "Where is it?"

Phil pointed uphill. "I think it must have fallen the other direction, and we were just confused." The fallen tree was indeed on the uphill side, and looked for all the world like it had fallen in that direction.

Franklin looked at Jeff, intensely serious. "All right, tell me. What just happened?"

"I asked Andar to move the tree for us," said Jeff. "And he did."

Franklin looked back at the fallen tree, got out of the bus, and looked again at the fallen wires. "Can he splice power lines?"

"I think that's our job", laughed Jeff. "Come on, let's keep going!"

The bus roared to life. "Hear that, Franklin? Sounds good, right? I drove out and back into the city yesterday, and out from the city this morning, and now up halfway to the dam, and guess what the gauge says?"

"The gauge says zero, Phil, I've been in your bus before!"

"Come look!"

Franklin grabbed the safety bar and stood over the driver's shoulder. "Full? It must be stuck there, just like it has been stuck on empty for years! Where did you buy gas in the city, by the way?"

Phil just waved a thumb over his shoulder at Jeff.

Franklin looked at him, waiting. Jeff just shrugged.

"Here it is," said Phil, turning the bus around a corner into a small parking lot below a high concrete wall. "At least, I don't know what else would be here that's as big as this."

He parked next to a small door hanging partway open.

They climbed down and looked into the door. Complete darkness greeted them.

Jeff felt the presence of something angry inside the structure. More than one something, in fact.

"Andar, if I go in, they will start tearing the place apart to throw things at me. If you go in, they won't bother with physical objects, so we won't make the repair problems any worse. Can you round them up, if I bind them?"

Andar was agreeable to that, so Jeff turned to the dam and spoke to the spiritual renegades who had taken it as their home. "I come on behalf of the King. Your time is over. Will you leave, or do we have to bind you up and carry you away to a place you don't want to be?"

A moment of silence followed.

"The place where your master waits."

A howl began, and seemed to echo through the internal structure of the dam, up and down all the stairwells, from deep underground to high above their heads. Phil and Franklin both covered their ears.

"Enough!" said Jeff. "Decide!"

The howl stopped.   Jeff could not feel their presence anymore, and he looked at Andar. The angel walked into the dam, not bothering with the door, and soon came out again, moving through the concrete walls as easily as the wind goes through the tree tops.

Jeff turned to the others. "I think they're gone, and Andar agrees. But there's still no light in there... "

"That book showed how they build dams, and I think there are enough windows at each level that we should be able to see... and climb the stairs... until the sun goes down." Franklin went to the door and walked a few steps in.

"It might work. Your eyes get used to it. But what are we looking for?"

"Maybe just anything that looks wrong... out of place, broken, falling apart ... breakers that have flipped. Loose wires."

"Phil, you're thinking like an Engineering Manager! Good work! You go first!" Franklin stepped back and bowed, waving Phil in.

"Andar, maybe your being in there would give us some light. Would you go first?"

He did, and it did. Soon they were in the control room, five stories above the ground level.

"See anything wrong?" asked Jeff.   "Shouldn't we hear something? Water flowing through, pushing things, gears turning, that sort of thing? I don't hear anything like that."

Everyone stood silent for a moment. There was a sound of water pouring through and falling down into the river below, but no sound of anything mechanical being turned by it.

"That's how the electricity is made, right? Water turns something, which spins wire loops inside magnets ... or the other way around... and that makes current in the wires... right?" Franklin waved his hands in the air, showing things turning.

"Yeah, I think so," said Phil, "but you just gave me the book today, and I haven't even had it in my hands yet!"

Jeff laughed. "I think that's right, my friends. Let's go find whatever should be turning."

They returned to the stair well, and walked carefully down nine flights to the bottom of the dam. Here the sound of water was quite loud, but still no metallic sound at all.

They stepped out into a wide, long space lined with enormous ... "turbines, I think they're called," said Franklin. The water ran in a wide channel between them, as though they should all have a hand in the water and be pushed to turn.

"Nothing is moving. Why?" Phil walked to the edge of the water channel and looked at the far side of the turbines. "It's like something has gotten stuck in their blades, but no tree trunk would be big enough to stop all of these, and I don't see anything."

"Maybe a safety valve, a shut off switch, something that just needs to be reset?" asked Jeff. "Like a breaker?"

Phil climbed some concrete steps up to a platform that looked out over the turbines.

"Whoo! You have not seen dust until you've seen this!
No one has been here since... well, you know." Jeff came up
beside him. Twenty feet of control panels stretched out
across the floor, with four rolling chairs that had not
rolled anytime recently.

Phil studied the switches. He took out a handkerchief and
began wiping dirt and cobwebs away from the lights and
handles. "I think I see something..."

Franklin came up beside him and watched.

"These all say, 'Main', and there's the same number of
these as there are turbines. And they are all in the 'OFF'
position."

He looked at the other two. "I say we turn one of them to
'ON', and see what happens!

He reached for the nearest one and pulled it towards
himself.

Nothing moved. He pulled harder. Still nothing moved.

He looked at the place where the handle went into the
desktop, and came away with a face like someone had replaced
his glass of water with vinegar.

"Oh, that's nasty. Something built a nest in there, and ... it
will need some cleaning. Let's try another one."

He stepped to the right, and pulled gently on the second
one. With a little jerk, it moved. He pulled it slowly towards
'ON', and the second turbine on the far side of the water
channel began to turn.

"Look!" said Franklin. "That's it!"

Phil got it all the way to 'ON', and let go of it. He was about to put his hand on the third one, and the second switch suddenly clanged back to 'OFF'. The turbine stopped turning.

They stood silent for a moment.

"Try the next one, Phil," said Jeff. "I can imagine there are loose wires, wires that have been chewed by animals, wires that are so corroded from time and mist that they barely carry electricity any more ... but maybe some of these will come on, and stay on!"

Phil moved from one to another, and in the end, five of the ten turbines were turning, lights were shining in the control room, and Phil had a good understanding of what needed to be done.

"I'll need to come back with some men and tools," he said, wiping his hands and putting his handkerchief back in his pocket. "They'll shut down again soon if we don't clean things up, tighten things, whatever. Doesn't take any book learning to get that far!"

"Bring lights when you come," said Jeff. "You want the power to be off, when you start working on wires."

"You know the best thing about all this?" asked Franklin.

Jeff smiled. "I think so."

"What," said Phil.

"The tree trunk is not blocking the road out!"

They rolled back into town at dusk.

"Nice," said Jeff, 'The way the park lights up at night."

"Yeah, I like .... What?" Phil stared out the window, and Franklin laughed.

"Good job, Engineering Manager!"

As they pulled up to the curb near Shady Bench, people ran over from all directions. "What happened?"

Franklin stepped down from the bus and waved his hands for people to be quiet.

"I'd like to introduce someone to you," he said. "Phil, would you join us?"

Phil carefully took the steps to the curb, and someone said, "That's Phil! We know him."

Franklin put an arm around his shoulder. "This is your new Engineering Manager. He has just repaired half of the electricity generation for the city, and will be looking for volunteers to go get the rest of it working!"

Phil was immediately covered up in eager helpers.

"But who will drive the bus?" asked Kenneth, tugging at Franklin's sleeve.

"Can you do it, Kenneth?"

"Me?"

"Sure. Can you do it?"

"If I do it, the bus will stop for breakfast every day at Johnson's place!"

Jeff smiled, and could see some of those new customers coming already.

Justice and Mercy

No More!

Alena stood with her back against the wall of the crumbling cement building as the angry crowd jostled past her.

"No!" they shouted, over and over. "No more!"

At the end of the block a platform stood in the intersection, and Alena moved slowly down the sidewalk towards it, close to the wall and out of the flow. Soon the streaming crowd changed from strong, fast walkers chanting loudly to older, slower people following along, not saying much. Alena fell in alongside a frail lady with a bright red cane and said, "Hi."

The cane came up across Alena's stomach. "Don't tell me what to do," said the lady, brushing Alena aside without looking at her, still pressing forward towards the platform.

Alena fell in behind her and saw the crowd had circled the platform, shouting their "No!" demand at three people who stood there without moving. Three tall men, all in black, with expressionless faces.

When the crowd had assembled and surrounded the platform, apparently streaming in from all directions, the man in the center of the platform raised his hand. Instantly silence fell, and no one moved. The three men moved to stand facing in three directions, their backs to one another.

"The leaders have been gone for a long time," said the man with his hand raised, "and we will now take their place. You will do as we say, as people always did for them."

Complete silence, until one voice rose from the other side of the platform to repeat the objection, "No!" But it was weak, and no others joined in.

The speaker pointed to that part of the crowd and said to one of his companions, "Mark him." The other simply nodded, and silence again was complete.

Alena moved through the crowd, instantly drawing the attention of the speaker. He stepped back and spoke quietly to the others, who came to his side.

She found the steps up to the platform and slowly climbed them, watching the men. They turned, always facing her, saying nothing.

When she stood on the platform, a slender figure barely 5 feet tall facing three large men, someone in the crowd asked, "What is she doing?"

"Getting herself killed," came the quiet answer, a whisper that easily carried to everyone in sight.

Alena spoke first. "Who are you?"

The men seemed to grow taller, and did not answer.

She spoke again. "What are you?"

The three men moved closer together, and appeared to merge into a single man, a towering giant of a man in black with no trace of a human expression on his face.

"Leave this city," she said, "and do not return." The man took a step towards her and began to snarl.

"Go," she added, in a voice as calm as when she began.

He stopped, grew wider and taller, and now did not appear at all like a man. His long arm reached out towards her.

"Now."

The arm pulled back, the "man" convulsed, and began to shout at her in words she did not understand.

She pointed at the thing and one more time, in a whisper, said "Now."

It exploded into fire and a swirling black smoke. A blue streak of flame raced into the sky, and the sound of the explosion echoed down the streets in every direction.

People slowly uncovered their ears and stared, as Alena stood alone before them and the smoke drifted away.

She turned slowly around, and after looking in all directions, began speaking.

"The King, whose name is Jesus, has set you free from the 'Leaders', those liars who controlled the lives of your ancestors for years. He invites you to meet Him, and to live in peace under His care. My name is Alena, and He sent me to give you that invitation."

After a moment, she added, "You will have many questions. I will answer as many as I can. There is no hurry. Everyone who wishes to go is free to do so. We can talk anytime you wish."

She walked to the edge of the platform, sat down with her feet off the edge, crossed her ankles, leaned back on her hands and waited.

The red cane pushed its way through the crowd and was firmly planted on the street. The lady carrying it took a stand before her.

"I'll start," she said. "Thank you for whatever you just did. That thing was awful." Many around her echoed the thanks.

"You're welcome," said Alena. "How can I help you?"

"Who are you, really?"

"Alena. Sent by the King, Jesus, to help clean up and put things back together. It's been a mess since the Battle, right?"

Heads nodded all over the crowd.

"So what still needs doing? Besides getting rid of things like that black creature, of course."

Conversations started here and there, and soon everyone was talking with their neighbors, many of them pointing at her as they talked.

"So who is this Jesus, this King? We've never had a king, and don't want one now!" The lady brandished the cane at Alena. "Had enough of people telling us what to do!"

"I'm sure you have. You are Eleanor?"

Eleanor stared, and lowered the cane. "Who told you that?"

"I think Jesus did. You weren't introducing yourself, so I asked Him."

"Since my mom passed, no one on this earth knows that name for me," said Eleanor. "Ellie, if you please."

"Glad to meet you, Ellie. You're my first friend in this city!"

"Sorry I hit you back there," she mumbled, waving back down the street. "I was angry."

"You're forgiven. Oh, and that's the message everyone needs to hear."

She stood, and called out for the crowd to listen.

"The King has paid the price for all your wrongs, and all the wrongs done to you. Forgiveness needs to be your way of life, from today on. If someone does wrong, we can deal with that, but put away from you all the darkness ... hatred, envy, greed, bitterness, resentment, all of it. Forgive!"

She looked around. "Got that?"

"What does it mean, 'we can deal with that'?" shouted a man at the edge of the crowd behind Ellie. "Are you a judge, or something?"

"Come talk with me later," said Alena after a quiet moment. "The King is telling me what's behind your question, and we can talk about it."

"That's nonsense!" he shouted. "You have no idea who I am!"

"Well, let's see..." she said, and was quiet for a moment longer. "How much do you want me to say, while everyone is listening? Geraldo Sinclair, I think, an attorney — or used to be — you live on 17th near the bridge, you have two sons ... shall I go on?"

"No," he said, much more quietly. "I'll see you later."

"That will be fine." She raised her voice, turning slowly to look at everyone as she spoke. "Forgiveness is yours, if you'll give your life to the King. He has already given his life for you. I'll tell you more about Him, as the days go by, and I hope you will love Him like I do. You can speak to Him anytime you wish. He's here as well."

She sat back down. "Ellie, why do you have a cane?"

"You know that man's name, and mine too, but you don't know why I have a cane?"

"I only know what He tells me."

"It hurts to walk."

"Where is the pain?"

Ellie pointed to her right hip. Alena pushed off, and dropped down to stand on the street. She offered to put a hand on Ellie's hip, and looked at her.

"May I?"

"Do what? It hurts!"

"Ask Jesus to heal you."

"Do anything you want, just don't push on it!"

Alena set her hand on Ellie's waist, closed her eyes, and spoke softly. After a moment, she looked up.

"Ellie ... there's something you'll need to give up."

Ellie stared, and her eyes narrowed. "I got no money to give you!"

Alena laughed. "No, my friend, not that." Seriously, then, she added quietly, "Your mother. Forgive her."

Ellie closed her eyes, clenched them tight, and trembled. "That's too hard."

"When you're ready," said Alena, and stepped back. "When you're ready."

Geraldo

The next morning, Alena sat by the fountain near the bridge and waited for Geraldo. He came from the old brick building with file cabinets in the windows, and hurried up the street to meet her.

"Can we talk here? It's nice," she said, and stood to offer her hand.

He looked around, shrugged, and shook hands with her. He sat heavily on the bench, and she resumed her seat, leaning against old bricks and watching the water play on the aging statue of a Roman lady.

"We have no judges," said Geraldo. He stared at the fountain. "No laws, no enforcement of laws ... it's all gone. Nobody wants what we had under the 'Leaders', and no one remembers how such things were handled before that."

Alena nodded, and waited.

"So some take advantage of others. Some are bullies. There's no ... there are no rules to go by, no protection for the weak ones. And no one to enforce them, if there were."

She nodded again. "What do you suggest?"

"Me?" He looked at her. "Seems to me you just took over the city. The whole country, for all I know. What do YOU suggest? What did you mean when you said, 'we'll take care of it', or some such?"

She traced a pattern on the stone bench, and said nothing. Finally she looked up. "If I wanted to talk about everything from here to the sea coast, and up to the river that comes across from the west and goes to the sea, and all the way west to the mountain range ... what would I call it?"

"Were you listening to me?" he demanded.

"Yes. What would I call this area?"

"Maybe 'Texas.' Sort of. With a few adjustments... the mountains collapsed, new ones rose up, everything changed, but that used to be the right name. The river you described is still in the same place... mostly..."

"How many cities are in 'Texas'?"

"Hundreds, I suppose, if you count all the small ones... and what's left of the big ones."

"Do they all have the same problem you just described?"

Geraldo rubbed his face, and turned to sit squarely facing her. "Probably so. What is your point?"

"Do you want to solve the problem just for this city, or for all of them?"

Now Geraldo began running his finger across the concrete bench, and seemed to be placing cities, thinking about borders, and considering the question.

"All of them," he said when he finally looked up. "How would that be possible?"

"Depends. What would you consider a 'solution'? What would that look like?"

"Safety. Peace in the streets. Agreements that could be relied on. Physical protection from bullies, and from attacks, whatever, that might come from outside, from other places."

"Let's just work inside those borders. Other people are working 'outside'."

He stared at her. "People like you?"

She nodded.

After a moment, he relaxed and leaned back again. "Okay. Just for Texas. What do we do?"

"It seems like laws would be the answer, but that's always been God's second choice. He much prefers a living relationship with each person, and that's my goal. Starting with you, actually."

She turned to face him.

"I think you are a big piece of what He wants to do here, but first ... you need to know Him."

"So introduce me. You said he was here."

"He made the earth we sit on, the stars above it, and every creature you've ever seen. He hears your words, even your thoughts and the intentions of your heart. Yes, He is here."

"I don't see him."

She brushed the objection aside. "Think about it this way. A king comes to a beggar by the roadside, and has compassion on him. Chooses to adopt him, actually. So the king offers a trade: the beggar can receive the life of a king, with full rights to everything the king has; but the king will take everything the beggar has, in exchange."

"That's everything for nothing. That's ridiculous. Any beggar would take that offer!"

"So you'll do it? Give everything you have, including your very life? If the King gives his very life to you, in exchange?"

They looked at each other for several minutes. Alena watched his eyes, and felt the struggle going on inside him.

She pressed harder. "It's not easy, I know. It means serving Him, not yourself. Doing things His way, not yours. Letting things remain unsolved, if He does not solve them, and focusing on things He considers important, whether you do or not."

"Why would new laws not work?" he groaned, leaning over and staring at the pavement under his feet.

"We have a little time ... a few hundred years, I think ... before the Liar comes back. Anyone who refuses the King, anyone who does not really know Him by that time, will be deceived and swept away. Our goal ... my goal, for Him ... is to bring everyone to Him, before that time."

"That's a much bigger goal that what I asked for!" he exclaimed. "Much bigger!"

"But it's the only way to reach your goal as well ... solving the problem in the heart, not just in people's actions."

"In the hearts of all those people? Is that what you're saying?" He stood up, and waved around in all directions. "All those thousands of people... maybe millions?"

"We should get started," she smiled. "Are you ready?"

"Aaaaghh! You're crazy!" he shouted, and collapsed back onto the bench.

"You need to meet Him," she laughed, "and then you can complain to Him about me being crazy. Are you ready?"

"Is the beggar ready to give his life to the King?"

"Yes," she said, "exactly."

It seemed to Alena that most of an hour went by before Geraldo turned slowly to look at her, and with tears in his eyes, whispered, "I've done it. And He accepted."

Alena jumped up, spun around, took Geraldo by both hands, and danced around him. "Yes!" she said, and laughed, and shouted, "Yes!" again. They both laughed, and danced a circle or two, then stopped. Geraldo wiped his face and let out a long, slow sigh.

"Thank you... Alena. Thank you. Now what?"

You Want Justice?

Two weeks later Alena and Geraldo went to the platform at the center of town, and set up a table on it with two chairs. When a crowd had gathered, Alena announced that they were there to receive requests and make decisions.

"Make decisions?" asked a man in the crowd. "Who made you a judge?"

"I am here on behalf of the King, my friend. Mr. Sinclair" ... she nodded to him ... "asked in our first meeting how this would work. We are about to find out."

They sat down at the table and waited.

"How can we do this?" Geraldo asked quietly. "No law, no principles to guide the decisions, no enforcement of anything we say ... how does this work?"

"Let's find out," said Alena. "In every situation, we'll ask Him what to do. You, too!" she laughed, as he raised his eyebrows. "Yes, we ... we ... both of us."

He looked at the couple coming up the steps, and took a deep breath.

"You know Him, now," she whispered. "They're coming to Him, not us."

He nodded slowly. "OK, OK, I got it..."

"Martin," said the young man. Motioning to the young lady by his side, he said, "Susanna."

Alena waited. When nothing more was said, she asked, "We are here for the King. What have you brought to Him? Do you bring a question, a problem, a gift, or something else?"

"A simple request, ma'am. Sir." Martin nodded to Geraldo. "Would you marry us?"

Alena smiled. "What a wonderful request, to be so simple. Is that your desire also?" She waited for Susanna to speak.

"Yes," said Susanna. "But my parents would say, 'No.'"

"Are they here?"

Susanna nodded, and pointed into the crowd. "Invite them to come up," said Alena. "And yours, Martin?"

"I am alone, ma'am."

While her parents came towards the steps, Alena asked Martin, "Can you take care of her? Do you have income, a home, some substance?"

"No," he said, "I have nothing much. And they'll tell you that when they get here!"

"So what will you do, so you both have food and shelter?"

"Anything I have to. I am strong, and have some skill with tools."

Geraldo stood up. "I need someone to repair my office building, and several others besides. Are you available?"

Martin stared at him.

"Steady pay," said Geraldo, "and you'll be working for the King."

Martin nodded. "Yes, sir... yes, thank you."

Geraldo sat back down. Susanna's parents came to stand next to her.

"Welcome," said Alena. "You object to Martin and Susanna being married?"

"Yes!" said the father, red-faced after climbing the steps. "He has come after her without my permission! He's a bum, no job, nothing!"

"Your daughter is lovely, sir. Can you forgive him for wanting to marry her?"

"No! He should have asked!"

"Then neither does the King forgive your many sins. As for his ability to support her, Martin has a job that will last for years. Mr. Sinclair has hired him. You may go."

The father stared at her, and then at Geraldo, who simply nodded.

Alena continued. "Since you do not approve, Stewart, please step down so we can proceed with the wedding."

"What? What?" he blustered, as his wife took his sleeve and pulled him backwards all the way to the stairs, then turned him and pushed him down to the street. When he was safely down, she turned and came back up to the platform. Without a word, she came to Susanna and hugged her, then hugged Martin. With tears in her eyes, she bowed slightly to Alena, then returned to stand at her husband's side in the crowd.

"Does anyone else object?" asked Alena. Martin and Susanna looked at each other, then together said, "No."

Raising her voice, Alena spoke so the whole crowd could hear. "In the name of Jesus, the King, I declare you, Martin and Susanna, to be husband and wife, and command that all here present do everything in their power to support and protect this union. Go in peace, to love and serve each other, and to honor the King in everything you do."

After they had hugged, said their thanks, and were about to leave, Geraldo spoke up.

"Martin."

"Yes, sir?"

"I don't expect to see you for at least a couple of weeks! But when you've settled in, come see me. You know the place?"

"Yes, Mr. Sinclair, I do."

"Bring your tools, and here's something to help you celebrate in the meantime." He held out his hand and dropped something into Martin's open palm. "The King bless you."

When they had gone, Geraldo whispered to Alena, "I think He was telling me the same thing. The words were in my mind. Was that His voice?"

"I suppose so," she said, "and since we walk by faith — which means, we never know for sure — it's important that you tell me, and that I tell you, when we hear something different!"

The next people to come to their table were two men, standing somewhat apart and obviously unhappy with each other.

Alena nodded to Geraldo. He stood up and faced the men.

"What is it?"

"I am Gustav," said the tall, blond man in the dark clothes of a businessman. "He is the problem!" Pointing to the frail, older man, he frowned. "This worthless fellow is living in my building, and paying me nothing. And he will not leave!"

"And your name?" asked Geraldo, turning to the other man.

"Simmons, sir. And he has no one else waiting to live there. And I just live in one room. And I have nowhere else to go."

Simmons looked at Gustav, with sadness in his eyes. "And it has been my family's home for hundreds of years."

The crowd around them was silent.

Geraldo looked at Alena, and she just sat there, looking back at him.

Finally he asked, "How does it happen to be your building, Gustav, if it belonged to his family for that long?"

"The Leaders gave it to my family, and thus to me."

"They took it from him, and gave it to your family? Was Mr. Simmons, or his family, paid for it?"

Gustav shrugged. "Doesn't matter."

"Mr. Simmons, was anyone ever paid for the building?"

The old fellow shook his head and said nothing.

Geraldo looked back at Alena. "I believe this is stolen property, and should be returned to the rightful owner."

Alena nodded, and simply said, "So decreed, by order of the King."

Both of the men before them stood silently, as though unable to believe what had just happened.

"Mr. Simmons, the whole building is yours, completely yours. You may do with it what you wish," explained Geraldo. "And Mr. Gustav, since you have expressed some animosity towards Mr. Simmons, you are not to enter the property ever again, or threaten him in any way. Is that clear?"

Turning to Alena, he added, "With your approval?"

Alena nodded. "You may go, gentlemen."

Simmons thanked them and quickly left, but Gustav stood there, exclaiming "You cannot do this!" and shaking his finger at them. "I won't let you do this! I demand justice here! That property was given to me!"

Alena looked up at Geraldo. "Is the King telling you anything about the other properties Mr. Gustav holds?"

Geraldo was silent for a moment, then said, "I think it numbers... in the hundreds of properties!"

"Is that right, sir?" asked Alena.

Gustav did not speak, but the look on his face told them it was true.

"What else do we know about Mr. Gustav, Geraldo?"

"Since you demand justice, Gustav," said Geraldo, with his eyes closed and brow furrowed, "I believe the King would like to address the matter of your partner ... a Mr. Sams? ... Who disappeared suddenly, some years ago?"

Gustav's face paled, his eyes grew wide, and his mouth slowly fell open.

"Yes, Mr. Gustav?" said Alena. "What can you tell us about your partner?"

"And are you sure you want justice?" she added quietly.

First Day on the Job

"Why did you hire me?" asked Martin, when he came to the office to meet Geraldo. "You don't know me at all. That was kind of sudden, wasn't it?"

Geraldo nodded, and eased down into the chair behind his cluttered, worn desk.

"Was I right? Will I be glad I did that?"

Martin smiled. "Yes, sir, you will. I promise. But I do have a question."

"Another one?" laughed Geraldo. "Go ahead! I expect a few hundred!"

"What do you want me to do? Maybe I don't know how!"

"How old were you, when everyone went off to the battle?"

"Nine, sir."

"And pretty much every one that was older is gone, true? Except a few of us, who couldn't go for some reason."

"Yes. I suppose that's right. My brother was just fourteen, and they made him go."

"So everyone who really knew how to do everything... they're all gone. So we all have to learn how to do everything, again ... everything that's needed."

Geraldo waited for that to run around in Martin's brain for a minute.

"Maybe the question is, what do you want to learn to do? Because everything needs doing! Sit down, please, we're not in a hurry."

Martin looked around and found a chair that was mostly empty. He moved the stack of books to the edge of a nearby table, and pulled the chair towards Geraldo's desk.

"Well... what's on the list? I can use carpenter tools ... all the hand stuff, since electric tools aren't much use the way the power comes and goes."

"How were you and Susanna going to live, with no job and no support from her father? I assume you've gotten a place to stay, with what I gave you."

"Yes, we found a place. Thank you. Umm ... not sure. Just knew we wanted to solve that puzzle together. And I'm pretty good with puzzles, actually."

"Really?" Geraldo leaned forward. "Good with numbers, and figuring things out?"

"You bet, sir. Much better with numbers than with a hand saw! But there's that one puzzle still on my mind..."

"Sorry. I didn't answer, did I?"

"No, sir, not yet!"

"The King that Alena talks about. He told me to. And since He knows you better than you know yourself, I'm pretty comfortable it will work out."

"How does he know me?" frowned Martin. "I've never seen him. Never even heard of him, before all this started."

"You've seen Him. Remember the battle, before all the screens went dark?"

"I do! They always say it was aliens out of the sky, led by someone wearing crowns."

"That was Him, the one who destroyed the Leaders. They had wiped out all knowledge of Him from this world, and now He is sending people like Alena to introduce us to Him again."

Martin sat back and stared at him. "That ... and you know him?"

"Would you like to meet him?"

"I'd be terrified! That was horrible, what he did!"

"Getting rid of the Leaders?"

"Well ... that was a good thing, sure."

"And telling your father to move out of the way, and telling Alena to marry you two?"

"Those ... those were good things."

"And telling me to hire you?"

Martin nodded. "Same thing. But ..."

"Long before that battle, He was tortured and murdered by the Liar, the one behind those 'Leaders'. He let it happen, to clear the way for you to know Him now, and in fact, to become His brother. Like I did, about a month ago. He's good, Martin. Very good. And if you'll give your life to Him, like I gave Him mine... He'll give you life that lasts forever. Like the life you see in Alena."

"Whooo." Martin stared at the ceiling. "Amazing what can happen, in your first day on a job!"

They both laughed.

"Think about it, my friend. And call me Geraldo, not 'sir'. I threw away all my ties a long, long time ago!"

"Yes, sir. I mean... OK. But what is a 'tie'?"

The next day, Geraldo took Martin to a large room almost filled with a broad table, and spread out the drawings of the building they sat in.

"There are people who want to start new things, new businesses. They'll make and sell things that people need, and that way they can have some money to take care of their own families. Right?"

"Yes, sir. Sorry. Yes, Geraldo, I understand."

"And we can help them. I have lots of rooms here, but they'll need electricity for lights, and we'll need working bathrooms, that sort of thing."

"Do you have good electricity here?" asked Martin.

"It comes to the outside pole, most of the time. But in all the earthquakes, the building was damaged, and has never been repaired. At least it was not crushed or destroyed, like most of them."

Martin nodded.

"So we can make room for people, but the wiring and pipes need to be working. We'll probably have to tear into the walls to find things, and fix things... but these drawings show what should be there."

They looked over the plans for a few minutes.

"I think I see what's there, and where to look," said Martin. "Do you mind if I damage the walls to do the repairs?"

"When you're done, we'll fix the walls. Do what you have to ... if you're in doubt, take a moment, turn your mind to the

King, ask what to do, and see if an answer comes clear in your mind. If you come to me, that's what I'll be doing as well, so, you might was well save the time and do it yourself!"

"He'll talk to me like that?"

"Why not?" laughed Geraldo. "Alena told me a story of how He used a donkey one time, to straighten somebody out. So I guess we're no harder to talk to than that poor beast!"

Alena appeared at the door.

"Welcome, my friend!" said Geraldo. "I think Mr. Martin has everything under control here. Something else I can do for you?"

"Glad to see you getting busy, Martin. Everything all right at home?"

"Yes, ma'am, we're fine, and thank you again."

"Well, then, I'll take Geraldo and leave you to the work."

Clearing a Nest

They walked out to the street, and Alena led the way towards the outskirts of town.

"Are we going far?" asked Geraldo.

"Yes, but not on foot. There's a man named Philip who was transported 'by the Spirit' to a place where he was needed, in the days after the King first walked the earth, and I think you're about to experience that. Something's going on about a hundred miles west of here, and I'd like you to go with me."

As she talked, a cloud gathered around them, and Geraldo could not see her, much less the road or the buildings around them. When it cleared a moment later, everything had changed. He stopped walking, and looked around. The crumbling remains of a small town surrounded them, with a one-story shopping center a few hundred yards ahead. The building seemed to cover an entire block, and had a higher ceiling on the left end. A second story, or three, just in one part?

"What do you see?"

"No one," he replied. "A deserted town, perhaps still damaged from all the upheavals."

"Now close your eyes," she said, "and tell me what you see."

He smiled. "It's getting harder to be surprised by anything you say!" He closed his eyes, and the shopping center suddenly took the focus of his mind, and it was the only thing he saw.

"Can you see inside it?" she asked.

He began looking more intently at it, all just in his mind. Without noticing, he began walking towards it.

"Yes..."

"And?"

"Darkness. Almost a solid black, more than just not having the lights on."

"You can open your eyes," she said, poking him. "Would not want you to trip over anything!"

He looked down, and saw that he was about to run into a curb. They stopped walking.

"What's going on?" he said quietly, as though the building could hear him. "What's in there?"

"The Liar is locked up, and the 'Leaders' are gone, but that still leaves a lot of their ... how to say it? ... 'spiritual followers' still on the loose. I think we've found a nest."

"What can we do?"

"First, know that you have authority over them. I do, as a representative of the king, and now you do too. As He directs, you can speak in His name also."

Geraldo stared at the building, and it seemed to stare right back, and somehow be getting bigger.

"I wouldn't know what to say. 'Leave...'"?

"We have a little help with us. His name is Renus. You should be able to sense him here, even if you don't actually see him."

"Oh!" exclaimed Geraldo. "He's right there, next to you!"

"Very good. He'll go with us, and I doubt anything there would give him much trouble."

She began walking steadily towards the building, and Geraldo hurried to catch up.

"Oh, sorry!" she laughed. "His legs are longer than ours!"

The building seemed to lean into them as they drew closer, as though it were pushing back, pushing them away. A cold fear ran down Geraldo's back, and a sudden, overwhelming desire to turn and run.

Alena put a hand on his arm, and it surprised him, as though coming out of a dream.

"Focus," she said. "It's a lie, don't believe it. Reject the fear."

He looked at the building again, shook himself, and set his jaw. "I reject you," he whispered.

The sky was clear. The building was normal. Everything was fine. They could go back home now. He started to suggest that to Alena.

"Again," she said. "It's a lie. Look as you did before, and don't let them play with your mind."

Once more he set his jaw, determined to not be a toy in their hands.

They approached the front door, tall glass doors that used to invite people in out of the sun and weather. Strange that glass doors would be so black, he thought. I should be able to see the hallways inside ...

Alena pulled on the handle, and it might as well have been set in cement. She stepped back. "Renus?"

The angelic presence moved to the doors and they exploded inward. When the boom had echoed down the corridors and back out again, and the flying glass had all fallen to the floors, they stood looking in.

The hallways were clear and brightly lit. The darkness must have just been the glass?

He looked at Alena, and she smiled.

"OK, I get it," he laughed. "Now what?"

"They're hiding. Let's go find them."

"Good thing they built high ceilings," exclaimed Geraldo, looking up. "Renus would have a problem." A smile seemed to radiate from the angel as he walked past them and a low-hanging, dusty sign for mattresses and pillows crashed to the floor.

At the intersection of the hallways, they caught up with Renus.

"Which way?" asked Alena and Geraldo at the same time. Renus moved to the left, and they followed.

At the end of the hall, past dozens of rooms filled with leftover evidence of stores suddenly deserted, was another set of glass doors into what must have been the 'anchor,' the store around which the mall had been built.

Again, the glass was black, and Geraldo fought to reject the fear and pressure that hammered on him as they approached it.

"You feel the attack?" asked Alena.

He nodded, not quite able to speak.

"Tell them to stop it."

He stared at her, then turned to look at the doors. Renus backed up a few paces and stood behind them.

"You ... stop it," he mumbled. Nothing changed.

He looked at Alena, and she simply raised her eyebrows at him.

He turned back to the doors. "We are here in the name of the King ... stop the attack."

Nothing changed. He began to be angry.

"Stop it!" he shouted.

Suddenly it was gone. The glass cleared, and Alena put a hand on the door and easily opened it.

"Congratulations," she smiled. "Shall we go in?"

They stepped onto a carpet that used to be a dark forest green, under the layers of dust and scattered debris. Ahead was a circular stage filling the middle of the room, with chairs facing it on all sides. People filled the stage, but not willingly. They were crowded together, some collapsed, some asleep, many lying on top of others as though they had been poured into a container with invisible walls, and could not get out. They appeared dazed, weary, and exhausted.

As Geraldo and Alena walked towards them, a man noticed them, and as he raised a hand to point, he leaned forward and fell off the stage. A tall man behind him fell forward into the suddenly empty space, staggered through the invisible wall that was no longer there, and fell on top of the first man.

"Stop!" commanded Alena. "Look at me!"

Dozens of faces, seemingly half-conscious, turned towards her and slowly focused their attention. "Where are you?" said one. "Who is that? I can't see you," said another.

"Do not move!" shouted Alena. "We will bring you out, one by one!"

Those closest to the ones who had fallen began moving towards the edge, pointing at the ones on the floor.

"Stop!" repeated Geraldo, coming to the foot of the stage. "Wait!"

He lifted the men from the floor and gently started them walking up an aisle, out of the way for others to follow. He then motioned to the next person, helped them down, and then the next. Alena approached the stage from the next aisle between seats, and began doing the same.

"Please sit down," they repeated, over and over, as they helped people off the stage and into the aisles of chairs. Many stumbled, seemingly weary and barely conscious, and some appeared to be blind.

When all had been moved down into chairs, they sat staring at Alena and Geraldo, or at least towards the voices. One by one, questions began.

"Who are you?"

"Where did they go?

"How did you break the wall?"

"Why can't I see you?"

"How long have we been here?"

"Listen to me," said Alena, and the voices quieted. "I see that you have been badly treated, and perhaps are starving.

The darkness that was holding you is gone, and you will now be free. If you cannot see, or you have been injured physically, please raise your hand. We will ask God to heal you, and do whatever else we can. Everyone else, please relax and wait while we help your friends."

An hour later they had prayed for all who needed healing, and it seemed everyone could see again. Geraldo asked the next question: "The town looks empty. Does anyone know where we could find food and water for you?"

"My store is two blocks away, and I had some things in the back. Corn, rice, beans, whatever. Maybe it is still there. They destroyed everything in the front when they came."

"The bakery at the other end of this building might have bottles of water left..."

"My house is close by ... We can do some cooking there..."

Geraldo took the storekeeper and some helpers to look for supplies, and Alena asked some to go with her to bring water back. "Everyone else, please wait here so we can get water to you quickly, then we'll go fix a meal and have time to talk. It looks like there are bathrooms in the wall behind me, so use them as you need to."

"But will the dark things come back, if you leave?" The small lady seemed almost terrified at the thought, and her voice was shaking. Alena looked toward the back of the room. "Renus, you will remain with them?" He smiled and nodded.

"You will be fine," Alena reassured them. "You have a friend here who stands before the throne of God, and nothing of the darkness will be able to enter past him!"

People looked around, trying to find their new friend, and half a dozen pointed to him. "He's right there, isn't he!"

"Yes," laughed Geraldo. "He is right there. I see God has been at work in some of you already. Be at peace, and we'll be back soon."

The search teams were soon back carrying boxes full of bottles of juice and water, and sacks of food supplies. "Who has a house big enough to cook for this crowd?" asked Alena, and the house that had been offered turned out to be quite large enough.

Before sundown, the survivors were all fed and were slowly recovering from their captivity. Several were sleeping, but others were ready to talk.

"How long were you held there?" asked Geraldo.

"The light in the high windows went dark, and then light again, at least 10 times. Maybe two weeks?" suggested a young man lying in the corner of the room. "I never realized being able to lie down would feel so good."

"Could you see the ones that held you there?" asked Alena. "What did they look like?"

Several began talking at once. "They were just shadows ... Sometimes they had bodies, but not always ... Their eyes were terrifying ... I couldn't tell if it was one or a thousand ... "

"I'm sorry," said Alena. "We were in the city about a hundred miles east of here, and we came as soon as the King sent us."

They began talking among themselves. "What 'king'? There's no king!" "Who is she talking about? ... "They walked a hundred miles?" ... "How did they break that wall?" ...

"First things first," laughed Alena. "Everyone who could see where Renus was, back in the auditorium, come gather around me."

Seven came forward and introduced themselves. Jonathan, the youth from the corner; Lynne, slender and perhaps 70; Rasco, her husband, with a quick smile and a little grey hair left; Conrad, the shopkeeper; Lewis, tall, still shaky, but able to walk; 'Stretch', even taller, and eager to understand; and Sally, in whose home they had gathered.

"When I spoke with Renus, you saw or felt where he was, right?"

They nodded, and some said, "I think so!"

"When we prayed for you, the King touched you, and began making you able to see things of His kingdom. I think that means you can also hear His voice in your heart and mind, and begin to walk with Him, be led by Him. Renus is an angel, and no man can see him unless God gives that ability."

She waited for some reaction.

Jonathan raised his hand. "Ma'am? He's over there behind you now, right?"

Alena looked back. "Yes, Jonathan. Can everyone else tell that he's there?"

She saw they were hesitating. "Just to give you confidence that this is not your imagination, let's ask him to move, and you can tell me where he goes."

She waited a moment. "All right, where is he?"

"Maybe, the same place?" asked Sally after a long silence.

Alena looked back and laughed. "Renus, are you playing with them?"

"Yes," she said to Sally. "All right, does everyone agree? He did not move?"

Heads nodded, and there were embarrassed laughs by those who were sure they had been wrong.

Alena looked back again. "All right, now where is he?"

But she did not need to ask, because all seven of her students were looking up at the ceiling, and then turned to look at the other side of the room.

"Convinced? Now, more important is that you can learn to hear the voice of the King, and that you can lead others to him. I'm going to pray for you, and then I want you to look around the room and go to someone you don't know very well. Ask God to tell you something about them... Something you could not have known, maybe something they need prayer for. Ask them if you've heard God correctly. If you get it wrong, there's no problem, this is a new thing you're learning to do."

She paused, then continued. "And if there's something they'd like God to do for them, go ahead and pray. Just talk to God, who is our real Father, the giver of all good gifts, and ask Him to provide what they need."

She looked around, and all seemed ready.

"My goal is that you will lead others to Him for the rest of your lives, and teach them to do the same. Beginning with everyone else in this room!   Tomorrow, after everyone has slept, I'll tell you much more about what this is all about."

They nodded, looking very unsure about all this.

"Father," she said quietly, "You know everyone here, and all their needs. I bring them to you, and ask that you pour out your Spirit in this room, heal the wounds of the evil one, and lead all of these people into a new life with You. In the name of the King, I present them to you."

She looked around the room and laughed. "He's ready if you are!"

After a mountain of pancakes had been consumed the next morning, everyone settled in, eager to know what they had now been introduced into.

"But first," said Alena, "what happened when you prayed for each other last night?"

Everyone wanted to talk at once, and the stories were wonderful. But finally they were ready to hear what she had to tell them.

"Centuries ago, God came into the world as a man, to do what only a man could do -- reclaim the authority over creation that the original man had given away, show us who He really is, and pay the price for our deep and awful rebellion against Him."

"The man's name is Jesus."

Looks of recognition came over some faces. "That's not just a fairy tale, a legend? Didn't they kill him?"

She nodded. "Tortured and killed Him. But that was the price He paid, on our behalf. Only an innocent man could pay the redemption of a guilty man, much less all guilty men... And only God himself could become that man and pay that price."

"How can we know him, then? He's dead."

"I know the battle at Armageddon was much more recent, but do you remember the kingly figure that led the army on white horses, and destroyed all the armies assembled there?"

They did.

"Three days after they murdered Him, on the day celebrated for millennia as "Easter", he returned, and His resurrection is the proof that God Himself was at work. He is the king, and He is the one who sent me to you. He is the one who set you free yesterday, and who restored your sight. He is very much alive. And now, you know Him too! You just told me so!"

1000 Years

The King Wins, Right?

Jose silently appeared on the sidewalk at dawn, in front of the four-story brick apartments where many of his friends lived. Flowers bloomed in many window boxes, and the sidewalks were clean and in good repair.

We've come a long way, he thought. Settled cities, working economy, healthy and prosperous people around the world. Even that dream that could never be achieved by human fantasy, "peace on earth."

But now... Major areas in quiet rebellion, looking for a chance to throw off the King's rule. How many will endure, in what comes next?

"Jose, what's on your mind?"

The voice came from behind him, but he knew who it was.

"Stan!" he said, turning. "A good night on the moonlight shift?"

"Yeah," he replied, setting down a bag of tools. "Things are running well, people like what we make, everything's good. But ... you look worried. Never seen you worried before. Talk to me."

Jose pointed across the street. "Coffee? Something that pretends to be breakfast, before you crash?"

"Sure!" Stan tossed his tool bag over his shoulder. "You're paying, right?"

"Like I always do."

"You never pay! What ... oh, I get it. Yeah, like you always do. Good enough for me!"

They reached the doors just as Tommy was pulling down the "Closed" sign. He pushed the door open for them, and a dozen early customers filed in behind them.

"Isn't it nice to not have to lock anything?" said Tommy, as he waved them in. "I don't think it used to be that way!"

They sat at the table and benches at the end of the row, next to the glass. "Stan looks hungry," laughed Jose. "Got anything he might eat?"

"Is there anything he won't eat?"

Stan shook his head. "As long as there's coffee, I'm up for whatever you need to use up!"

"I'll see what I've got too much of!" said Tommy, turning away and setting chairs down at the tables.

Stan waited, as Jose stared out the window. Finally, Jose turned to him. 'I've been Home."

"Thought so."

"It's almost time."

"For ... what?" asked Stan, leaning forward.

"We've known since the battle, centuries ago, that the Liar would be released again, for a brief time, to gather an enormous army and try once more to annihilate God's people."

"Where? How?"

"When the King showed all of that to John, he wrote that the Liar would deceive 'the nations of the earth, Gog and Magog,' with their armies like the sands of the sea, and march on 'the camp of the saints and the beloved city,' which I think means Jerusalem."

"Who are Gog and Magog?" asked Stan. "Never heard of them."

"I don't know," said Jose, "but John also said they would come 'from the four corners of the earth', so perhaps the meaning is that he will deceive all he can, turn them into enemies of God, enemies of the King, and try to destroy everything and everyone he can before his own end."

Tommy returned to slide a plate full of pancakes in front of Stan, and grab a bottle of syrup from the next table. "On your tab, Jose, as usual?"

"Can we do that, Tommy?"

Tommy nodded, and said "Forever. Will that be long enough?"

"That should cover it, I think," said Jose with a wink.

"The king wins, right?" Stan looked worried.

"Thank you, Stan. That's a good summary. Yes, the King wins. And much more. After this final battle, there is a white throne waiting, all will be judged, and this earth ... this universe... will be replaced with a new earth, new everything."

"So ... why are you worried?"

"How many of those millions who have believed us and committed to the King will endure? And how many will join those armies, and be destroyed?"

There was a long silence.

"That last time he was loose, it was awful, right? Horrible?"

Jose nodded. "Beyond description."

"But there have been people like you all over the earth, bringing us back to know the King. So everyone has been warned. Everyone has been prepared."

"Yes," said Jose, watching people stream by the window on their way to jobs, families, whatever they had chosen. "That's the goal. That's been our goal for a thousand years. What happens next is between them and God."

He stood up. "Enjoy your coffee, and try to finish breakfast before it's time for lunch! I need to go. There are things left to be done."

"Thank you," said Stan. "For everything."

Jose nodded, and was gone.

Ruso

Ruso stood from his throne, red-faced and furious.

"Get out!" he exploded at the young man before him. "Get out, with your talk of the king you admire so much! Leave my people alone with that nonsense. If I could kill you where you stand, I would have done it already!"

He looked around at the court full of silent watchers.

"Does anyone here disagree with me?" he demanded.

Complete silence was his answer.

"I want more than that! Who in this room agrees with me, and demands, by my side, that this arrogant ambassador of his so-called King should get out of our faces and never be seen again?"

A swell of approval ran through the crowded room.

"What did you say?" he cried out. "I couldn't hear you!"

The people roared their approval, with repeated chants of "Make him go, make him go, make him go!"

After several minutes Ruso sat back down.

"Now get out of here," he repeated to the man standing calm and silent before him. "You heard them."

The man turned slowly around, looking at the gathered witnesses. "Yes, I hear you," he said softly, and his words seemed to hang in the silence, clear as the song of a whippoorwill at dawn. "And so does the King. Be sure of your choice, each of you. Everyone stands alone when judgement begins."

Then he was gone. He did not leave, he did not walk away, he did not say farewell. He simply was there one moment, and the next moment not.

A slender, tall man in a red robe entered the room, and his shoes made no sound on the marble floor. Something about him drew all eyes to him, as he slowly approached the throne and stood before Ruso.

"Your majesty," he said, bowing.

After a moment Ruso shook himself, as though to come back from thoughts that were far away, and responded. "Who are you?"

"Who I am really does not matter, Majesty. I have something to offer. An opportunity you may like."

Those around began murmuring, and Ruso held up a hand for silence. "Well, then, person whose name does not matter ... what do you offer?"

"The so-called king you were just discussing will be coming to Jerusalem in three months' time, and many of those who claim to follow him will gather for the event."

The man in red looked around the room, then continued. "It will be a chance to destroy him, and all these fools that have been prancing about 'in his name' ..."

Ruso narrowed his eyes and looked very closely at the man's face, but could read no emotion there. "What reason do you have, to bring such an offer?"

"He has been some trouble to me as well, in the past, and I would be glad to settle matters. I could deal with him, while you clean up the followers. Do you have an army worth the name?"

"I do," said Ruso. "And I have a friend with another, just as big. Our soldiers together outnumber the sands of the sea."

"I thought as much," responded the visitor. "Your fame is widespread." He bowed to Ruso. "I will leave you to gather and prepare them. It will take a month to travel there, so you should be ready to leave in sixty days. We will meet again."

Then, almost as an afterthought, the man added, "I will speak with your friend as well. I know of the man, and I believe he will be glad to join us."

Without waiting permission to leave, the stranger turned and silently walked out.

When he had gone, Ruso turned to the viceroy at his side. "Did you notice ... his boots made no sound?"

"I did," responded the official. "With your leave, I will follow him and learn more about where he is from, and who he really is."

"Do that."

But the viceroy returned ten minutes later to report there was no trace of the man, and no one outside had seen him enter or leave.

Are We Agreed?

Charlman stood on the balcony a hundred feet above the gardens, and looked out over the smooth, grassy field and the forests beyond. The wide balcony, with its hanging lamps and a strong, polished floor, had hosted gatherings of two hundred or more for dinner and dancing long into the night. The alcove at the far end provided room for musicians and actors, and his guests had come to expect extravagant luxury at his parties.

But tonight he was alone, and as the evening light faded the stars began to appear, and the lights of the homes in town glowed across the forest two miles away.

This is not enough, he thought. I can ride across my lands in just five days, with the fastest horses man has ever owned. I need five times that. Twenty times that. I should have everything from here to the mountains on the west, and to the ocean on the east. Who deserves it more? Who can rule this land better than I?

And finally the thought formed. Why should I not just take it?

"You are welcome to do so," said the quiet voice at the balcony's entrance.

Charlman looked back. His soldiers were not there, for some reason he did not know. A man in red stood alone, and neither introduced himself nor approached.

"To do what?" asked Charlman, irritated at the interruption. "And who brought you up here?"

"To do what you wish," replied the man, ignoring the other question. "To take the land you desire, from the mountains to the ocean. And more, if you like. There is much more land to the north, between here and the frozen plains you would not care for."

Charlman slowly turned to fully face the visitor, but did not invite him closer. Something about him was unpleasant, but Charlman could not point to it, exactly.

"How do you know what I wish?" he said quietly.

"Am I right?" the man replied, with no explanation.

"Yes..." replied Charlman, the word coming out before he had actually decided to speak. "What is it to you?"

"What is it that restrains you?"

What, indeed? The question caused him to stop and think. Finally it was clear in his mind.

"These wandering messengers of the so-called 'king', I suppose. They stand against such desires, such possibilities, and I think three or four of them would oppose my movement in this matter."

Charlman began to be irritated at the way the conversation was being managed, and at not knowing who this visitor, the uninvited invader was.

"We can deal with them."

"We?" said Charlman. "Who are you, and who is 'we'? And who let you come up here, again?"

"Ruso and I will come against the king, when he arrives in Jerusalem in ninety days. You should join us. Together we can destroy him and all these followers his ambassadors have gathered."

Charlman stared at him.

"With them gone ... it is all yours," continued the visitor. "Are we agreed?"

Charlman could not find the words to respond. This insane man was reading his thoughts, answering no questions, and expecting him to commit a huge effort with no more foundation than his word.

"I will speak with Ruso," he finally answered.

"Prepare your men to leave in six weeks, to arrive at the appointed time. If you decide not to go, then I will give all this land we discussed, including the land you now hold, to Ruso. After we dispose of the pretend king, all of that will be in my power."

"This is nonsense," said Charlman, turning to look out at the horizon and think about the distance involved. It would, indeed, require ten weeks to move the army that far. "Who are you? Why should I believe any of this?"

There was no answer, and when he turned to look at the man again, no one was there.

To Jerusalem

The night before Ruso was to begin the journey taking his massive army to Jerusalem, he gathered his officers for dinner in the castle.

When the servants had placed venison and beef on the table and retired to prepare the second course, the man in red stood before them.

Conversation stopped as all became aware of the uninvited guest. He stood at the foot of the table, facing Ruso at the other end.

"You have done well to trust me," he said. "There is one thing more. The people at Jerusalem will have no weapons, so your men need not bother with shields and such. Make your trip lighter. Swords and lances will be all you need, and provision to carry much treasure when you return."

Ruso stood, and was about to speak when the man said simply, "I will meet with you on the way," and was gone.

Ruso sat down, staring at the place where the man had stood. The word "treasure" began to drift around the table as the officers resumed their conversations with one another.

Epilogue

And when the thousand years are ended, Satan will be released from his prison and will come out to deceive the nations that are at the four corners of the earth, Gog and Magog, to gather them for battle; their number is like the sand of the sea.

And they marched up over the broad plain of the earth and surrounded the camp of the saints and the beloved city, but fire came down from heaven and consumed them, and the devil who had deceived them was thrown into the lake of fire and sulfur where the beast and the false prophet were, and they will be tormented day and night forever and ever.

Then I saw a great white throne and him who was seated on it. From his presence earth and sky fled away, and no place was found for them. And I saw the dead, great and small, standing before the throne, and books were opened. Then another book was opened, which is the book of life. And the dead were judged by what was written in the books, according to what they had done....

And if anyone's name was not found written in the book of life, he was thrown into the lake of fire.

Revelation 20:7-15, English Standard Version